PORTRAITS OF AN
ADVENTURIST

JOE JESIMIEL OGBE

PORTRAITS OF AN ADVENTURIST

⟶ *Dedication* ⟵

To survivors of the

COVID-19 pandemic.

All across the world, the COVID-19 pandemic has left on its heels several stories; some tragic, and others pathetic. This adventure presents tales from a traveller who was locked down in a foreign land. His experiences are breath-taking and worth reading...

CHAPTER

One

My wife, Philomena and I arrived Tamale; the capital of Northern Region of Ghana, late in the night. The journey from Makayili was long, strenuous and very stressful too, especially for my wife who was pregnant. We were both very tired and exhausted when we finally got home. In an instant, I got hot water for my lovely heart-throb to have her bath while I chose to shower with cold water.

My wife felt she was not in the mood to eat any food. She said all she wanted was to sleep, but I felt otherwise. I urged her to eat some food no matter how little, but she refused. Instead, she tried to convince me why she didn't need to eat food at that period of the night.

She said, "My dear, please allow me to sleep. I'm tired. It's late. Don't you know it is past 11 p.m.?"

"I know," I responded, feeling somewhat sympathetic over her condition. "But apart from the snack you took on our way, you haven't taken any solid food. A pregnant woman must not starve herself, you know! My boy needs food, you know," I insisted, jokingly.

"No. Thanks my dear."

"At least, just a few slices of bread and a cup of tea will be okay."

"Okay! Okay my dear, if you insist."

"I insist!"

Within a few minutes, we had our late-night meal and went to bed.

Around 3 a.m. in the early hours of the morning, I woke up to ease myself. As I stepped out of our room, I saw a giant python trudging toward me. I quickly dashed back into the room, panting heavily as if I had encountered a monster.

In fear, I banged the door behind me. My wife woke up.

"What is it, my dear?" She asked in a state of bewilderment and shock.

"I saw a big python."

"What! Python! In this house?"

"Yes."

"What do we do?"

"We will kill it."

"How?"

"Don't bother how!"

"Okay. My dear, please be careful."

Quickly, I mobilised my brothers to assist me to kill the venomous creature. We searched the whole compound for the snake, but to no avail. All of a sudden, Johnson my younger brother, notorious for killing reptiles, shouted as if he was bitten by the snake.

"I have seen it. It's inside the big clay pot," he screamed, pointing to the vessel.

"Let's go after it," I instructed.

We killed the dangerous reptile. My brother was very happy, as he was going to prepare a snake cuisine.

Like Ugandans, we Ghanaians too love to eat snake meat.

I came back to the room to break the good news to my wife.

"My damsel, we have killed the snake," I announced jubilantly with my hands lifted in the air.

"Wow! That's great!"

"But I can't sleep again."

"Me too... I don't feel like sleeping."

"Good for us!" I giggled.

"Ahh! Don't be mischievous! Don't be naughty! I'm still tired..."

"My dear, do you know that since you got pregnant, our sex life has been suffering?"

"I don't think so. Yes, it's not been regular. But is sex your food?"

"Yes! It is an emotional food for a married couple! I'm beginning to think that pregnancy is a death sentence to our physical intimacy."

"God forbid... My dear, why do you think like that?"

"It's because of your uncompromising stance. You don't always respond to my sexual moves with excitement. You always say you're tired or you're not in the mood."

"I'm sorry. I don't mean to... My dear, let me be very transparent with you; these days, I get worried that we might be hurting our baby through sex... I'm struggling with changing sex drive. I want less sex! My mind is full of all manner of things..."

"So why did you bottle up your feelings till now?" I interjected.

"I have been afraid of your reaction, like how you'll take it, and stuff like that."

"Why will you be afraid of my reaction?"

"I don't know."

"To be honest with you, I want to have more of you now than when you were not pregnant."

"Wow, that's nice. I used to think I'm ugly for you, with a big nose, big lips, big everything..."

"Don't bother yourself about all that. I'm not complaining. Can we try to find new and more satisfying ways to resolve this issue?"

"How?"

"By talking more frankly... eh, more freely and being more open-minded about this and other issues. Okay?"

"Okay."

We discussed for over one hour. Our discussion helped to allay her fears. We ended up going all the way and satisfying each other, consummating our energies in a loving tango through the serene night.

At about 7:45 a.m. in the morning, I went to my mother's apartment to check up on her. As soon as she saw me, she brightened up and I greeted her.

"Good morning Mama! How was your night?"

"Good morning my son. My night was not good. I did not sleep well. I even became like an owl that does not sleep at night."

"What happened, Mama?" I asked.

"My waist was hurting me. I also coughed throughout the night. My enemies are after me..."

"Mama, your enemies are not after you. You need medical attention urgently," I interjected.

"Not now. I will be fine."

"Mama, you are not fine. It's very unusual for you to still be in bed at this time."

"What time is it?"

I looked at my wrist-watch and responded, "A few minutes to 8 a.m. Mama."

My aged mother, Mrs Janet Abdulai, stretched out on the bed and coughed. I promptly assisted her to sit up.

"Mama, sorry. Take it easy. You will be fine. Do you have any cough syrup?"

"Yes."

"Where is it?"

"Check that container." She pointed at the container on the centre table which had 'seen many years'. I picked the bottle of cough syrup, shook it vigorously and administered it to her like a trained nurse.

"Mama, for how long have you been taking this cough medicine?" I asked.

"For about three or four days. I don't know why I'm still coughing this much."

"You should have gotten better by now."

"I don't know, maybe the drug is even fake. My son, these days we have more fake products than original products. What about your wife?"

"She's getting dressed. She'll be here any moment."

"Okay. It will be nice to see her. Congratulations; I learnt that she is pregnant. Thanks be to God."

"Yes! She is six or seven months gone..."

"That means she will soon deliver. Two or three months to go for her?"

"Yes! God is good! Mama, I'm travelling to Accra next week ... I'm actually going to Lagos in Nigeria for training."

"My son, it is too early to go for any training. Your wife's condition requires your presence. You need to be around her."

"Mama, I know, but this training is very crucial for my advancement in life. I brought my wife to stay with you for motherly care and support."

"Okay. I will do that free of charge," she responded in a weak voice.

"Is your wife in support of your trip to Lagos?"

"Yes Mama."

"But you just got married and you are travelling to Nigeria, leaving your wife behind. You are meant to stay with her, at least for one year before talking of travelling... She will miss you."

"Don't worry Mama, I will miss her too... But Mama, I'm not comfortable with your ill-health."

"I will be fine. My sickness is only nocturnal. Day time, I'll be strong as a lioness but in the night time, I'll be as weak as a weakling."

Both of us chuckled.

In a moment, my wife walked in and greeted, "Good morning Mama."

"Good morning, my daughter. How was your night?"

"Fine Mama. And you?"

"Ummm, I'm much better this morning."

"We arrived late in the night and we felt it will be improper to disturb you."

"Ahh, you should have come, my daughter. I was not even sleeping."

"Ahh, we didn't know, Mama. My husband and his brothers killed a giant snake in this compound."

"Snake?"

"Yes, Mama. They even broke your clay water pot."

"Mama, it was a great deliverance for me," I chipped in. "The Python could have attacked and bitten me if not for divine protection."

"Oh my God! No evil will befall you, my son."

My wife and I responded with a loud 'Amen!'

"Have you taken breakfast?"

"Yes Mama!" I answered.

A week later, I was set to embark on my journey to Accra. My wife prepared a sumptuous breakfast of fried plantain and egg stew for me. We ate together with great relish. Mom came out of her room and proclaimed blessings on me for my journey. She signaled her intention to accompany my wife and me to the motor park, but I tried to dissuade her, "Mama, don't bother coming..."

"Why?"

"Your ill-health, Mama."

"No sickness and nobody can stop me from seeing my son off to the park."

"Okay Mama! Let's go then..."

At the park, there were many touts 'hunting' for passengers. Two of them scooted toward me, wanting to snatch my luggage. The tall, huge one yanked the luggage from me and said, "Oga, my vehicle is clean and neat for you."

"No, bros, my own is fully equipped with an air conditioner. It's a long journey from here to Accra. Sir, you need to be comfortable," the second tout said.

"No! He is lying. Come and see..."

They engaged each other in a mild scuffle.

"What's going on here?" I yelled at them. "Please leave my bag alone... I will decide the vehicle I want to board... leave me alone!"

My plea fell on deaf ears as both of them were still arguing and struggling with each other. Finally, I decided to go with a 7-seater Toyota Sienna van; 2015 Executive Model.

I held my wife in an affectionate, warm embrace. She started sobbing. My Mom joined her to sob. When I saw the tears of the two most important women in my life, I became emotional as I could not control my tears anymore. I allowed tears to drop while trying to console both my wife and mother.

A few minutes later, the large-framed tout asked me to sit in the front seat with the driver. Upon entering the van, I remembered that I had not given enough money to my wife. I quickly alighted from the vehicle and implored the driver to wait.

"Please, just a minute."

I walked briskly toward my wife and handed her some amount.

"More money?" She asked.

"Yes, you will need more money. You know we are expecting..."

I gave her a hug again and ran back into the van, waving to her and Mom. They waved back too, my wife doing so joyfully, but Mom, with a snivelling look.

The driver asked me to pray before our departure.

"Mr Man, you look like a pastor. Please pray for us before we start this journey."

After a short but powerful prayer, the driver drove slowly out of the park and entered into the major road to Accra.

A Kilometre or two from the park, a haggard-looking Police Officer who might have been suffering from a hangover commanded the driver to stop.

"Stop there. If you move, I will move you with my rifle... settle... settle us now!" He said authoritatively.

"Okay! Oga Officer!" The driver squeezed a few wads of Cedis into his hand.

"Carry go!" The officer instructed.

Not too far from the first police checkpoint, the driver was stopped again at another police checkpoint. This time, we were asked to disembark for security checks. And as we were about filing out, the driver told us not to bother as he was going to 'settle' the officers as usual. He alighted from his van; walked a few metres to 'settle' the officers and we were allowed to go.

"Settlement is the language on Tamale-Accra road. No van or bus passes without settlement. That's Ghana for you! Settlement! Settlement everywhere," the driver lamented.

"But you drivers are to be blamed too," one passenger, a middle-aged man said, curtly. "The giver and the receiver of bribes are equally blameworthy."

"No! No! We are not culpable... They are law-enforcement officers and we can never refuse them except you don't want to ply this road."

"Corruption is a major challenge in Ghana!" Another passenger said, matter-of-factly.

"Do you know why corruption is endemic in the Police Force?"

"I don't want to know. But come to think of it, there is no justifiable reason for bribe-taking in the Police Force."

"Their salary is very poor. They are poorly paid!" The first passenger opined again.

"They are not the only ones in service that are poorly paid, my friend."

"I still insist that poor remuneration can engender corruption."

Another passenger, an elderly woman contributed a comment. She said, "I'm a retired policewoman. And I can tell you that the poor remuneration in the Police Force is prompted by bad leadership."

"Madam, there is no good leadership in our country as a whole," I responded to her comment.

"Ummm, it is true! " The driver consented.

"The rot in the Police Force is a reflection of the society. A corrupt society will breed corrupt policemen," I retorted.

"I don't agree with you at all!" The retired policewoman responded angrily. "...It is not a societal problem but a leadership problem. Good leadership can change society. Leadership is everything..."

A fair-complexioned passenger interrupted, "Let's leave police matter, they are corrupt beyond redemption. No reason is potent enough to justify their corrupt actions."

"If I were in government I would deal with the police top brass, as they are the promoters of corruption in the system..." The retired police woman opined again.

"Yes, yes Madam, I agree totally with you..." I said, to concur.

"Until corruption is curbed within the top echelon of the force, police officers will continue to take bribes on the road," the woman said. "Yes, I can tell you that our top officers are helplessly corrupt. Do you know that we only enjoy good postings by lobbying our seniors? It is a 'man-know-man' situation, not by merit," she submitted.

"But Madam, why do you people have dirty barracks? It's an eyesore. Visit any Police Barracks, and you will know the true meaning of the word – dilapidation,"

I opined.

"Your observation is very true. Our bosses mismanage or out-rightly steal the money meant for the rehabilitation of police barracks..."

"My people, my own problem is the bad road! Our government is corrupt for not fixing this road, " the driver contended.

Virtually all of us in the vehicle joined the driver to castigate and condemn the Ghanaian government for neglecting the ever-busy Tamale-Accra road. Ghanaian roads, like other African roads, were crumbling faster than they could be fixed. For a first-time traveller on the road, this could be a major source of extreme frustration. But old-time travellers on the road might never be bothered as they were used to the sorry-state of the road. But for goodness sake, how could one be used to bad roads? Ghana! Ghana! My Ghana!

All of a sudden, the driver mistakenly drove into a ditch-like pot-hole and he shouted: "Oh, my shock absorbers!"

"Sorry about that, " I consoled him.

The driver drove gently from the main road and parked by the roadside to observe the noise he was hearing from underneath the van. The bumpy and dusty road had nearly damaged his van.

Fortunately though, he was spared a major expense at the motor mechanic shop, as there was no vitiation.

We bounced back on our journey.

Few hours into the trip, virtually all the passengers were asleep. But the driver kept himself awake by eating kola nut. To him, long journeys would require chewing gum or kola nut. As such, he was busy doing justice to his kola nut. He offered me some but I declined his offer.

Then he jokingly said, "See your eyes like that of owls..."

"Are you insulting me?" I inquired.

"No. Not at all Sir. It's because you are not asleep like others. I eat a lot of kola nuts to keep myself awake. It is my insurance against sleep."

I giggled and said, "For goodness sake, how could kola nut stop you from sleeping? Do you have any scientific evidence?"

"Oga passenger, I have experience. I'm a long-distance driver, that's what I chew to keep me awake and agile throughout my journeys."

"Hmm, I wish you the best of luck, driver."

"Thank you!"

The driver murmured to himself which filtered to my hearing. He said, "If not for the bad road and the police 'stop and search,' I would have been in Accra since. A journey of five or six hours is taking me eight hours. What a country! But I still thank God, today's trip is better. The other day, the journey was an unfortunate one, as we slept overnight on the road."

Upon our arrival at the Accra-Tamale motor park, I alighted from the van with other passengers. In a moment, I picked a cab to my friend's office.

CHAPTER
Two

I alighted from the red cab that brought me from Accra-Tamale motor-park, I thanked the cab driver and walked briskly towards the office building. Immediately, I was accosted by a hefty, smart and dark-complexion security man.

"Hello, young man! Who are you? And what's your mission here?" The man asked me.

"Good evening Sir. My name is Pumaya Abdulai.

I'm here to see my friend," I answered rather courteously.

"Who is your friend?"

"Moses Leke-Ayua by name, Sir."

"Okay! We know the young man. He is a good guy.

Do you know his office? He's on the 4th floor, Room7!"

I said, "Yes Sir," and tried to move away.

Courteously, the security man said, "You just have to fill the visitor's form first before you proceed further. Okay?"

"Okay Sir."

I was handed a form which I hurriedly filled and gave back to another security officer at the post. As I was about stepping out toward the elevator, another security personnel, this time, a female officer who was wearing dark glasses, stopped me and demanded to know the content of my bag.

"Mr Man, what do you have in your bag?" She inquired.

"Nothing much. Just my personal effects, Madam."

"Open the bag for search!" She demanded.

"Why not, Madam."

As I was about opening my bag, the male Security Officer made a sign to his female colleague to stop the search. Motioning toward me, he said, "Don't bother opening."

"Thank you Sir."

I carried my bag and hurriedly entered the elevator.

Meanwhile, my bosom friend Moses had been expecting me, even to the point of getting worried. Moses' dark solemn face was tilted towards the door at the point I was ushered in by his female secretary. Moses wore a black T-shirt on blue jeans. He had an air of dignity about him.

"Pumaya! What kept you this late?" He asked.

"We had so much traffic challenge from the motor park to this place."

"I guessed as much. This is the rush hour when many workers are rushing back home from the office. Please sit down."

"Thank you."

"Was the journey hectic and stressful?"

"Not really. We arrived Accra on time. But the journey from the park to your office was something else."

"Umm, you're welcome! How's your wife?"

"My wife is doing great. She sends her greetings."

Moses' secretary came in with two bottles of malt drinks and snacks to offer me and her boss.

But Moses requested for coffee instead.

"Please give me coffee. I love coffee!"

"I know that about you. I like coffee. Maybe I have to drink coffee too, so I can be awake throughout the journey."

"Don't you think it's rather late to embark on this journey tonight? Why not sleepover in Accra and proceed first thing tomorrow morning? How about that?"

"But I like night journeys. The quietness of the night is simply nice. Do you know that most of my trips are done in the night? We have low traffic in the night, you know."

"Road Safety authorities do not subscribe to night-travel," Moses quickly chipped in. "Me too, I advise against it. I can't buy into you going tonight, my friend. Are you not exhausted from your journey?"

"Yes, I am."

"Then you sure need some rest."

"Advice well received! Let me rest in your house tonight."

"That's great. You will be refreshed, and tomorrow morning, you will be on your way to Lagos."

My telephone rang. I picked the call.

"Hello! Hello!" It was my wife calling.

"Hello, have you arrived?"

"Yes, my dearest damsel."

"Are you travelling tonight?" She asked, with much care and concern in her expression.

"Not at all. My friend, Moses has convinced me not to.
He advised that I sleep over at his place and have some
rest."

"That's nice of him. Nice friend, he is."

"Honey, my damsel, I miss you already. Talk to you
later."

"Miss you too. My regards to your friend. I love you."

"Love you too."

As we were about going home, my phone rang again.

"Hello! Hello! Who's this?" I inquired.

"It's me, your mother."

"Mama, good evening Ma. Why are you using an
unknown number to call me?"

"My phone battery went flat and my sister, Mama Koffi,
gave me hers to use. My son, how was your journey?"

"Fine Mama! Please, I will call you later in the night
since I'm no longer travelling tonight. I'm sleeping over
at my friend's house, Mama. He advised me not to travel
in the night because of the inherent danger."

"Okay my son. That's a good advice from a good friend.
Mama Koffi asked me to greet you. She also wants you
to visit Koffi in Lagos. Expecting your call. Bye-bye."

"Bye, Mama."

In a few minutes, the Uber driver arrived and he called to signify his presence.

"Let's get going," Moses said.

"Okay."

I picked my bulky travelling bag to follow Moses.

"Your bag is big. And you can even hide a full-grown man in it and nobody will know," Moses joked.

"Ahh, no, no, it is not possible..."

 We both chuckled as we hurried downstairs without using the elevator.

Moses turned to me and said, "I love using stairs quite often. It's good for bodily exercise, you know."

"Yes."

As soon as we came out of the office complex, the security man who was nice to me earlier on, approached Moses and asked, "Anything for the guys?"

"Nothing for you guys today. Is everyday Christmas? See you guys tomorrow," Moses responded.

"Okay Sir!"

Moses smiled as usual and we entered the waiting Uber car. The driver took an unfamiliar route. And Moses promptly challenged him, "Why are you taking this route?"

"Oga Sir, I just want to dodge traffic on Nkrumah Road," the driver replied.

"That's okay. Thank you for your knowledge of traffic situation in Accra."

"Thank you Sir."

"My pleasure."

"This driver is a good person for sure," I whispered to Moses.

"Yes, I presume. He is unlike others who would have loved to follow a traffic-infested route for personal gain."

"Some of these drivers are simply dubious and callous at times. They always like to take advantage of situations to cheat people, particularly if you don't know your bearing or where you are heading."

Within 15 minutes, we got home! Moses paid the fare. And in a jiffy, the driver zoomed off with his tyres screeching loudly.

"Do you know that this driver has saved me some cash? I would have paid much higher if he had taken Nkrumah Road," Moses said while opening the door.

"That's nice. These days of economic quagmire, every Ghanaian Cedi is a blessing."

Moses opened the door and we entered the living room. We were so tired and worn out.

"Welcome to my humble abode. Sweet home, I'm back home," Moses enthused.

"Beautiful and neat abode. I like your house."

"Thanks for your compliments."

After putting my bag on the centre table, I sat down on a beautiful white sofa. The choice of window curtains and colour of upholstery showed that Moses had good taste for Interior decor.

"Your living room is elegant and beautiful. I'm not surprised though. You have been a young man of taste. You've got a taste for beautiful things," I complimented Moses again.

"You too!"

I chuckled and said, "But yours is a higher grade!"

Moses joined in the laughter, and responded; "Higher or lower grade, let's just go and have our shower. And then I will take you out for dinner. Will that be okay?"

"That will be perfectly okay!"

After having our shower, it did not take us long to get dressed. Moses came out looking casual but sharply dressed in a pair of brown chino trousers and brown Italian slippers to match. It has become a tradition or lifestyle for him to always step out of his house smelling fresh. Today, he wore a Polo Blue perfume on his beautiful Polo-blue-striped T-shirt. I, on the other hand, was not particularly concerned about dressing. I wore the same dress that I wore from Tamale. As a young man on a mission, traversing several villages, my dress sense was nothing to write home about.

"I'm taking you to our usual joint. Do you like their food?" Moses asked.

"For sure, I like their food."

"Okay then, let's go right away."

We strolled casually towards Greatmeals Restaurant located at the extreme of Tankoni Street, chatting and laughing heartily.

CHAPTER
Three

Eating out in restaurants had become a delightsome pass-time for Moses, perhaps because of his bachelorhood. He fell in love with Greatmeals Restaurant, a popular Nigerian eatery that served local Nigerian cuisine. Most Nigerian nationals based in Accra always trooped to the restaurant to have their breakfast, lunch, and dinner.

To some Nigerian customers, eating in Greatmeals was like eating sumptuous Nigerian meals in the heart of Lagos. Moses would tell anybody who cared to listen that he was not missing Lagos, food-wise, and that was courtesy of Greatmeals Restaurant! According to him, one thing that kept pulling or attracting him to the restaurant was the Nigerian Art and Craft Interior.

As a lover and collector of Artworks, he knew the worth of those classical artworks which adorned their walls. He simply loved the ambience of the restaurant and also the first-class treatment which the restaurant offered her customers.

As soon as we arrived the restaurant, the personable waitresses that were usually positioned at the entrance promptly stepped forward to welcome us. A fair-complexion waitress offered to take us to a table meant for two guests; not too far from the garden.

Looking seductively into Moses' eyes with an enchanting smile, she courteously said: "Welcome again to Greatmeals where we serve our cherished customers the best of Nigerian dishes. Kindly have your seat."

We sat down and chorused, "Thank you."

"What type of drinks do you want? Beer, malt, juice or soft drinks?" The waitress asked.

"Give me orange juice and water, room temperature," Moses replied.

"What about food, Sir? We have pounded yam, garri, amala, and fufu. For protein to go with the soup of your choice, we have goat meat, beef, bokoto, assorted meat, dried fish and snail. There is also jollof rice, and fried rice served with salads or boiled yam, boiled potatoes, garnished with vegetables in chicken sauce or fish stew."

Moses, wearing his usual smiling face, responded with a question: "What type of soup do you have to go with the solid?"

"We have affang, edikaikong, egusi, vegetables, okro, and ogbonno soup, Sir."

"Please give me hot pounded yam with ogbonno soup. I want assorted meat to go with it. Okay?"

"Okay Sir."

The waitress turned to me and asked:"What would you like to eat? And drink?

"Same thing. Just give me what you are giving my friend."

"Okay Sir."

"My pleasure."

Within 12 minutes, our order was ready. Two waitresses brought our food and drinks on white trays; placed them on the table, and said simultaneously: "Enjoy your meal Sirs!"

After washing our hands properly, I offered a blessing on the food and we started eating. But Moses noticed that the quantity of soup served was not going to be sufficient for us. He called on the waitress that took our order and complained. But the waitress insisted that there was nothing she could do.

As we were arguing over the soup ration, a pretty young woman came to our table and introduced herself as the manager. On closer observation, she recognised Moses.

With a simple smile on her beautiful face, she said, "Oga customer. Thank you for your patronage."

"Good evening Ma'am."

"What's the issue Sir?"

"It's the issue of soup. I like plenty of soup, you know. Why do you people like serving me little soup? See how you are treating me, your regular customer. Do you want me to change camp?"

"Oga, no, no, don't change camp. I'm so sorry Sir. Please, let me add some more."

She walked briskly into the kitchen and brought some more soup. Moses thanked her and continued eating. He turned to me and asked, "Did you see courtesy in practicality?"

"Yes, my friend. I'm impressed!"

"I'm very impressed too! I'm over-flabbergasted!"

Commending the manager further, I said, "She is well cultured. See how she went to fetch more soup by herself! That's humility."

Moses, trying to clear his throat, took a glass of juice and opined, "This is why I love this eatery. The manager has a good understanding that the customer is king."

"Yes, the customer is king. You mistreat your customer to the peril of your business."

When we finished eating our meal, Moses called for the bill which he promptly settled. On our way out of the restaurant premises, some beautiful girlies were beckoning on us. One of them made every attempt to seduce us but we ignored her. Her dressing was nothing but complete nudity.

I stopped, trying to talk with the girl.

"What do you think you are doing? Let's keep going. Do you want to talk to her?" Moses questioned me.

"Yes, I want to preach the gospel to her."

"Preach to a prostitute at this time? It is 9 p.m. already! Pumaya, my reputation... if people see us, they will have an impression that we have come to pick them... this is risky!"

"But we can take this risk to save a life."

The girlie moved close to us and asked: "Hi, you want me? The night is 30!"

"30 what?"

"30 Cedis, for the night!"

"How are you?"

"I'm not okay. No business, no customer."

"Can I talk with you just for a few minutes?" I requested.

"About what?"

"About Love."

"Love? That's interesting..."

"God loves and delights in you, even though He does not delight in your trade."

"Mr Man, I'm not out for this. Please spare me..."

"God's love is superior to man's love. Please allow me to ..."

"To do what? To preach to me, when I'm here hustling to fend for myself and family? You are a bad market!" The young prostitute said angrily and backed off.

I followed her and tried to persuade her to give me audience, even if for a few minutes.

"Mr Man, leave me alone. I'm not prepared."

"Even if you don't want to hear my message, let me get to know you personally. You may need me sometime in the future. Let me have your phone number."

She reluctantly agreed, "This is my WhatsApp number!"

I wrote it down on a paper. She looked at me with suspicion. I offered her a gift of 30 Cedis and moved towards Moses, where he stood waiting.

When the girlie saw the money, she became relaxed and was now ready to listen. She followed me and appreciated me.

"Thank you for the gift."

"My pleasure. Do you know that Christ is the greatest gift given to humanity? I just gave you a gift. If you had rejected the gift, it would never benefit you. So also, Christ as a Gift of God will not benefit you if you reject Him. For whosoever shall call upon the name of the Lord shall be saved. Salvation is for whosoever! You can be that whosoever tonight ..."

She abruptly interrupted me, "Please, please stop. For your information, I used to be a Christian... I'm a backslider now. And I don't think God will have mercy on me. My sins are too much..."

"No sin is too much before God. He forgives all sins..."

Like a joke, she ran away into nihility.

We got home at 9:30 p.m. on the dot. We sat down discussing the young prostitute who just vanished into thin air.

"What do you make of the young lady's action? Why will she just run away from you like that?" Moses asked.

"I think she was completely overwhelmed with her iniquities. She could not face the truth of the gospel. Thank God I have her number. I will definitely look for her when I get back from Nigeria."

"Pumaya! I have been living here for nearly three years now, but I have never had the courage or temerity to share the gospel with those sex workers; members of the oldest profession ..."

"God loves them too..."

"Yes! Yes!"

"Let me go to bed early so I can make it early to the park."

"Okay! Good night, Pumaya."

"Good night, Moses! I deeply appreciate you for giving me a treat. It was such an outstanding outing. This experience will remain memorable for me to relish."

"My pleasure!"

CHAPTER
Four

I woke up feeling terrible, frightful and terrified because of the nightmare I had. Looking at the wall clock hanging directly opposite me, I noticed that it was 3:55 a.m.

I got up, buttoned my pyjamas and dashed hurriedly into Moses' room. Meanwhile, my friend was still fast asleep. I didn't know what to do, but I was wondering whether it was proper to wake Moses or not. In a moment, I reasoned and concluded that it was proper to wake him. But before I could attempt to do that, my friend woke up.

Wheezing heavily, I managed to greet him, "Moses, Good morning..."

"Good morning, Pumaya. Why are you up this early? Are you okay?"

"Not really. I had a nightmare."

"Nightmare?"

"Yes. A horrifying nightmare."

"Please sit down."

I sat down beside him on his wooden 'mazonia' bed, holding my head with my two hands as if my head was a heavy pot. Both of us kept silent for a few seconds and I started narrating my nightmare: "Moses, in the dream, I found myself in a hut without windows. How I got there I cannot remember or even describe. I saw terrifying human figures like young and old men crying! Some were wailing like women in a burial ground who had lost a beloved relative. Some others were in serious pains. They looked beaten and battered with swollen hands, legs and faces. Before I could realise it, the hut was filled with more figures. Some were changing colours, and some crawling. The place became heavily crowded and congested. And we were all sweating profusely..."

"Ahh! Ahh, terrible dream," Moses interrupted.

I broke Moses' comment with a louder exclamation and continued: "... I found myself completely sandwiched between two hefty figures, whose legs were bandaged. These guys were smelling like rotten eggs. They started pressing me against each other, and I cried out and shouted, 'Help, help, somebody help me! These notorious, hefty guys gave me a series of hot slaps which procured instant headache. My head became heavy and was hurting me so badly. I cried out some more but nobody cared about my cry for help. In my heart, I began praying for God's help and mercy. Then, all of a sudden, a giant looking creature with unusual huge wings came into the hut, pulled me up from them..."

"That must be an Angel!"

"I think so. But let me finish narrating the dream."

"Okay."

I continued, "... the figure used his finger to create an opening and pushed me out. Then, I started running with all my might. I looked back and saw some people in dark and red clothes chasing after me. I ran until I outran them. In another dream, I think it's like a dream within a dream. I saw myself in a place where there was a great commotion; something like a riot. I started running but not in a specific direction. A shadowy bald figure with a big grin appeared and lifted me off the road path and held me up in his hands. I don't know how long he held me up. I got frightened and started crying out hysterically until I woke up."

"For sure, these are terrifying nightmares," Moses said.

"Can you interpret them for me?" I asked, still terrified.

"Am I the Biblical Joseph?"

"Moses, you can be my Joseph..."

"I see victory through angelic intervention. That giant looking creature that came to rescue you might be an angel. It could also mean a great man with great influence will assist you in times of trouble or difficulty."

"I think so too. But do you advise me to still proceed on this trip? I'm afraid!"

"Yes. You can. Don't give in to fear! But let's pray about the dreams."

"Okay!"

After prayers, I was encouraged to proceed.

I boldly declared my faith, "I now have peace about the journey. I will go and come back safely."

"Yes! Yes! That's the spirit. No devil or his cohorts can stop you!" Moses emboldened me.

By 5a.m., I had my personal devotion, showered afterwards and dressed up. Moses called an Uber driver to pick me up to the park.

At the Accra-Lagos motor park, one luxurious bus was set to go but could not, as they needed one more passenger. Meanwhile, a motor tout fronting for Lagos bound buses was screaming and shouting to attract passengers, "Lagos! Lagos! We are ready to move. One more passenger, one more passenger to go."

I ran toward the bus, and the tout took my bag and said, "Come and pay your fare quick quick."

"How much is the fare?" I asked.

"200 Cedis!"

At the point of payment, I was asked to present my International passport.

"Ahh! I forgot it at home! What do I do now? Can't I travel without it?" I asked.

"No trouble, you can still travel but you will have to pay extra 50 Cedis."

"But I have my ECOWAS ID and my National ID."

"That won't do, we need your International passport or you pay the extra 50 Cedis," the transport company manager insisted.

I paid 250 Cedis and I was directed to my seat.

The bus took off by 6:20 a.m. It was a smooth drive from the park to Ghana-Togo border, where fierce looking Immigration and Customs Service Officers were on hand to search our bus. Officers were satisfied with the search and allowed us to go on our journey. I was dozing off intermittently. I was not awake to capture the beauty of nature along the express road. A co-passenger sitting beside me touched my hand and asked, "Are you ready to change some money? This is the place we change Ghanian Cedis to Nigerian Naira."

"Where are we?"

"At Seme border. This is the Benin Republic-Nigeria border!"

"What about the Togo-Benin border? Have we passed it?"

"Yes. You were sleeping, and I did not bother to disturb you."

"Umm, thank you. My brother, I had a rough night."

At the Seme border, we were given some time to take a walk in order to stretch our legs and to do little shopping. I was able to change some of my Cedis to Naira. There at the border, I bought a Nigerian SIM card with airtime and established communication with my wife and Moses.

From Seme border to Lagos, our vehicle was stopped several times by Customs, Police, Army and all kinds of Security Agencies. One disturbing thing about their operation was that they were all demanding bribes. I concluded in my mind that bribery or corruption was an

African problem. But, Nigeria's case was both gigantic
and unique for many reasons.

I alighted somewhere around Lagos State University
(LASU). I called my wife and Moses that I had arrived
Lagos safely. And they were glad to hear about my
safety. Moses advised me to call the director of training
to help me navigate my way to the Training Centre since
I was not familiar with Lagos. But before I could put a
call through to the director, a co-traveller, a young man
in his early twenties, who alighted at the same bus stop
approached me for a little financial support to add to
what he had, to get to his destination.

I promptly gave him 2,000 Naira. My act of benevolence
overwhelmed him so much that he couldn't but show
heart-felt gratitude. His excitement was palpable. He
said, "Thank you so much. I asked for little but you have
given me much. I'm grateful."

"My pleasure."

"Where are you going Sir?" He asked.

"I'm going to YDI Centre. I learnt it is along Isheri-Lasu
Express Road, Igando. Do you have an idea about the
place?"

"Yes, I do. I know the place. I have been there a couple
of times for training. Can I accompany you to YDI?

"For sure! You can... "

"After all, one good turn deserves another. You just helped me, now it's my turn to help you too."

"Thank you for your consideration."

"My pleasure Sir!"

My new friend flagged down a taxi.

"Where una dey go?" The taxi driver asked in pidgin English.

"Na YDI Centre we dey go," the young man replied in pidgin English.

"500 Naira!"

"Very expensive..."

"Oga na night be this."

"500 jalè!"

"Okay."

"Make una enter."

We boarded the rickety cab and within 20 minutes we were at YDI Centre, where our training was scheduled to hold.

CHAPTER

Five

After forty days of intensive training at the Young Disciples International (YDI) Centre, I decided to pay my cousin, Koffi a visit as his mother, Mama Koffi, my aunt had requested me to do. When I called Koffi to intimate him about my planned visit to his home, he was so enraptured. He suggested that I should use Uber instead of the yellow Lagos cabs or buses. He was of the opinion that Lagos buses could be dangerous to first-time visitors, as there were so many unpalatable stories of how some visitors were robbed violently and left stranded.

I called for an Uber driver, who arrived at YDI Centre on time. And before I boarded the Uber cab, I discreetly took the vehicle number and sent it to Koffi. As soon as we left the Centre, I remembered that I forgot my means of Identification, and so pleaded with the driver to drive me back to the hostel. He did without hesitation. I rushed to the hostel, picked my ID and off we departed again.

At about 5:43 p.m., I arrived safely at my destination, into the welcoming embrace of Koffi who was anxiously waiting outside their duplex house for me. We greeted each other warmly and I was ushered into their beautiful home. Koffi and Jumoke lived in an all en-suite duplex located in Lekki-Ajah area of Lagos, which was quite a far distance from Igando where I was staying.

Jumoke came downstairs to welcome me.

"Hi, Pumaya you are welcome."

With every sense of etiquette, I stood up and responded, "Thank you so much. I'm glad to see you. It's been quite an age."

"I'm very excited to see you too. The last time I saw you was when Koffi brought me to Ghana during our courtship days."

"Yes! That's over seven years ago! Just like yesterday!"

"Please have your seat."

"Oh, thanks. What about the children?" I asked.

"They are in their room upstairs. Let me go get them. Oh, not me. Koffi, you go fetch them while I serve our August visitor drinks..."

"Okay!" Koffi replied, as he ran upstairs.

Jumoke dashed hurriedly into the kitchen and within a few minutes, she brought assorted drinks and placed them on a beautiful ceramic table before me. She respectfully and courteously asked, "Please, which do you care for? Malt drink, red wine or orange juice?"

"I prefer the juice."

"Okay."

Meanwhile, Koffi was taking much time to bring their lovely children downstairs. There was no cause for alarm, as he needed to change their dresses to more presentable ones. He marched them to me and said, "My brother, behold the products of our marriage."

"Wow! You have lovely children here."

"Oh, thank you"

I drew the children closer and hugged them. They were so excited to see me. I guessed my cousin might have told them a lot about me.

"What's your name?" I asked the pretty girl.

"My name is Nana! What about you, uncle?"

"My name is Pumaya."

"But Dad told us you're uncle David..."

"Yes, that's my second name."

Turning to her younger brother, I asked, "What's your name?"

"My name is Timothy and I'm 4. My sister is 6. Uncle, how old are you?"

"That's nice. I'm in my late 30s."

"Uncle, what do you mean by late 30s?"

"Okay. Let me be specific. I'm 39 this year."

"Uncle, soon to be 40, you're old. You are older than my Dad. Yesterday was my birthday. And I had fun with my friends."

"So sorry I missed your birthday. Did you have real fun?"

"Yes, uncle! My Mom took me to Apapa Amusement Park."

"That's nice of your Mom. Did you really appreciate her for taking you out?"

"Yes, I did."

"When is Nana's birthday?" I asked, while still carrying Timothy on my laps.

"I can't remember, uncle. But I can guess, March..."

"Nana, what about your birthday?"

"My birthday?"

"Yes!" I responded, still playing with them.

"My birthday, my birthday is 4th March."

"Ahh! Your birthday is past," I responded with a smile.

"Yes, uncle."

Jumoke stood up and excused herself. She asked Nana to join her in the kitchen to prepare dinner.

Koffi started chatting with me, asking about the well-being of our people in Ghana.

"I'm sorry I could not come for your wedding. How is your wife?" Koffi asked.

"She is doing great. We are expecting our first baby."

"That's great. I'm happy for you both."

"Thank you... How's your marriage?"

"My marriage is not there yet. We are still parching. There are still lots of learning to do, with lots of work to do. We need your prayers."

"For sure, I will pray for your marriage."

"Thanks. How was your training?"

"Splendid."

"That's great!"

"We learnt a lot of things. One of our lecturers, Mr Jasper Okoko taught us how to engender harmony and bonding in marriage..."

Koffi chuckled.

"I'm interested in that... My wife and I need to bond more."

"Yes, you can. Why don't you join her in the kitchen and assist her..."

"But I don't know how to cook."

"Must you know how to cook before you assist your wife in the kitchen? As you assist her, you bond with her and you learn how to be a good cook. Start it right now. You just have to do it," I advised my childhood friend and cousin.

"But I'm keeping you company. Some other time I guess."

"No! Don't bother about me. I insist you go and assist her. The children can keep me company."

"Okay. If you insist. What channel do you prefer to watch?"

"I prefer TBN."

Koffi changed the channel from sports to TBN and headed to the kitchen.

Jumoke was pleasantly surprised to see her husband in the kitchen.

"What are you doing here? What's going on here?"

"I'm here to assist you," Koffi muttered with great trepidation.

"Please, I don't need your assistance. Please, go and stay with Pumaya. Please go."

"Mom! Mom, don't drive Dad away. Let him stay to help us. Mom, please, please allow Dad to stay," Nana pleaded. Her mother asked her to go upstairs. Nana left, feeling so upset. On seeing his sister running upstairs, Timothy left me and ran after her.

Jumoke allowed Koffi to stay with her in the kitchen but seizing the opportunity to unburden herself. "Koffi, marriage is designed to be enjoyed, not to be endured," she said with misty eyes. "... I have been enduring this marriage. Koffi, you have been a thorn in my flesh. We are not connecting the way we should. When last did you help me in this home?"

"But you know that the whole problem started after I lost my job ..."

"Your job loss is not the problem but the way you chose to manage it. Other men will bounce back. It's been two years of joblessness, two years of agony, two years of trauma..."

Koffi got angry over the comparison. "Please stop comparing me with other men. We are all individuals. Spare me, I'm different," he said, grudgingly.

Koffi wanted to go out of the kitchen. But his wife stopped him.

She held him by the wrist as he made to leave. And she said, "Let's talk. Don't use anger to cover up. We just have to talk."

"Let's talk later."

"No! Let's talk now or I will tell your cousin!" She threatened.

"Please, let's not wash our dirty linens in public," Koffi responded in anger.

"Look at the way you wasted your money on gambling. Look at the way you chased those little whores, even some of them had the courage to send me nasty messages. Just look at your alcohol problem. Truly, I'm sick and tired of your untoward behaviour. I'm beginning to think of divorce lately."

"Divorce?"

"Yes, divorce!"

"Ahh, it has not come to divorce. I know it's all my fault... and I accept full responsibility. I promise to turn a new leaf from now. I'm sorry for everything."

"Sorry without genuine change will not suffice."

"My dear wife, I will change..."

"Who is your dear wife?"

"You, of course!"

"I don't believe it. If I'm dear to you, you will not traumatise our marriage and me..."

"But do you know that marriage is real work? Anything of value in life is real work. I promise to work on our relationship. Let's become better partners as we both work on our relationship consciously and conscientiously."

"But you have been the one frustrating me. You are the problem..."

Reassuring his wife, Koffi said: "It is my choice to stay married and in love, no matter the challenge. Marriage is a choice, you know. As for me, I have chosen you for life. I view whatever is going on in our marriage as a process for growth. I view times of disagreement as a time for us to grow closer and a time to understand each other."

"You are a smooth talker, you can even sell ice to Eskimos!" Jumoke responded. "Dinner is ready. Please go get the kids for dinner."

As he was about stepping out, he turned to his wife, pleading: "Please, promise me you will not tell my cousin. Please!"

"On the account that you will change..."

"Yes, I will!"

He gave his wife a kiss, something he had not done for months, and he ran upstairs to announce to his kids that dinner was ready.

"Dinner is ready. Dinner is ready. Let's go have dinner," he announced.

Nana and Timothy jumped out of their room, repeatedly saying after their dad: "Dinner is ready. Dinner is ready."

"Nana, go back to your room and turn off your AC and TV. Don't get Mom angry."

"Daddy, please carry me," the little lad requested.

Timothy jumped into his Dad's arms, feeling so loved and excited.

The table was set for dinner at 7 p.m. Jumoke, while dishing food for her children, said: "It has become our family culture to eat dinner early. Pumaya, hope you like it."

"Yes, I do. I learnt late-night meals could cause indigestion that interferes with sound sleep."

"Yes! Not just indigestion. Even studies have shown that late-night food increases triglyceride levels, a type of fat found in one's blood. When you eat, your body converts any calories it doesn't use right away into triglycerides; and high levels may increase your risk of heart attack and stroke."

"Ahh, God forbid! Jumoke, did you read medicine or nutrition?" I asked with surprise on my face.

"No. Just personal studies and research."

"That's nice. I have learnt something new to take away to Ghana. I love eating at any time of the day. My wife used to join me sometimes. With this information, I promise to make amends."

"That will be awesome."

"Koffi... Pumaya. Please serve yourselves. Take as much ration as you can. We have more in the kitchen."

Koffi urged me to take the lead, "You are our guest, you go first and I follow; after all, you are my elder brother."

"Okay. Thank you for the honour."

I served myself and waited patiently for Koffi and his wife to serve theirs before eating.

"Ummm, this is delicious food. Ma'am, you cook so well," I commended.

"Thank you..."

"My wife is the number one cook in Africa," Koffi interjected proudly.

Timothy said, "Uncle, my Mom is a good cook."

"Yes, your Mom cooks well. She is excellent," I nodded in approval.

Jumoke snapped: "Tim ... Tim, where are your table manners?"

"Sorry, sorry Mom. But I was telling uncle that ..."

"Telling uncle what?... Keep quiet. Eat your food. You don't talk while eating."

The little boy started crying.

"Why are you crying?" His Mom inquired.

"Mom, you shouted at me..."

"Okay. I'm sorry for shouting at you. But don't talk while eating."

It was a pleasurable dinner experience. After the meal, Koffi and his daughter Nana helped to do the dishes, while Jumoke and Timothy stayed with me to keep me company.

She said, "Koffi told me about your training. Hope you are enjoying it."

"Yes. The course is an eye-opener. Highly impactful and very interesting."

"That's great."

Koffi and Nana came out of the kitchen to join us in the living room after they were done with the dishes. Jumoke stood up and ushered the children upstairs as Timothy was already feeling sleepy.

"Good night, Pumaya."

"Good night Ma'am and thank you for the dinner. Can't wait to tell my wife about your hospitality. Thank you again."

"My pleasure," she responded.

Koffi moved closer to me, and engaged me in a tete-a-tete.

"My brother, I'm happy to have you in our home."

"Same here. I'm happy to see you and your family. Your Mom insisted I must see you. That's why I'm here. We had a tight schedule at the Training Centre."

"I guessed as much. You've been here for how many days now?"

"For forty-one days."

"Wow. That's great... My mom loves me."

"Yes, she does."

"My brother, I have been through a lot. Since I got laid off, I have been through hell. For over two years now, all my attempt to secure another job has proved abortive."

"Ahh, what a stroke of hard luck!"

"Yes, it is bad luck indeed."

"But do they fire people like that in the Oil and Gas sector? I thought there is job security there."

"My brother, job-loss is a global phenomenon. The global economic crisis is plaguing nations and corporations worldwide..."

"Koffi, is it true that you have now become a chronic alcoholic?"

"Why are you asking? Did you hear anything?"

"From the grapevine... I heard that you are struggling with many vices."

Koffi relaxed on the soft sofa and said penitently, "My brother, I must be honest with you. I have issues. I have problems. When my company decided to downsize, it was unfortunate that I became a part of those that were asked to go, maybe because of my alcohol problem."

"But why? You were not like this in Ghana. Yes. Yes... Koffi, remember that we used to booze together then but not to the point of being drunk or even being referred to as an alcoholic..."

"My brother, when I was laid off, my problems multiplied, but I did not make it a news item as nobody in Ghana got wind of my joblessness or other problems."

"Who told you? It was a news item in Ghana! It certainly was, especially, within your family circles. We even knew when your wife took over as the breadwinner, providing for the needs of the family."

"I must confront her. She is taking our family issues to the outside world. Isn't she?"

"No. She is not. But you know how news flies around."

"But how did the news fly around?"

"I don't know."

Koffi continued with his conversation, "Pumaya, do you know that I felt insecure, frustrated and depressed? I even became emotionally and physically isolated from Jumoke. We were drifting apart..."

"Isolation or drifting apart was the result of your reckless living," I interrupted. "Why will you keep company with bad friends or bad influencers and expect the best from your woman? You can't be drinking in clubs and beer parlours and expect her to give you kudos..."

He was silent for a moment as if he was meditating over an important issue. Koffi tried to say something but couldn't form the right tenses immediately. My words were piercing his heart and he started sobbing like a bereaved woman.

"My brother, countless times, I was picked up by some neighbours or passers-by from gutters in a state of stupor, dead drunk. It became an embarrassment or headache to my wife," he finally said remorsefully, shaking his head to press home his feeling of guilt.

"I sympathize with your wife for putting up with your recklessness."

"Yes, I agree with you. She has tolerated my misdeeds for too long," Koffi said again in a shaky voice.

"Your wife has tried. Other women may not have tolerated your weaknesses."

"At some point, she opened up to some of her friends about her ordeal with me. Some even advised her to throw me out, while others advised her to be patient; that Rome was not built in a day... Do you know that when I left the company and was given a golden handshake, I ended up mismanaging the money?"

"What did you do with your money?"

"Womanizing, gambling and alcohol," he said. His face lit into amazement as to mean he was surprised this really happened to him.

"My brother, you were really foolish."

"Yes, I was. My wife advised me to invest, but that fell on deaf ears."

"You are even lucky that your wife did not throw you out of her life."

"She contemplated divorce a number of times, but her major hurdle was her parents. She knew that her parents would not support her, hence she did not push for a divorce..."

"What did she decide to do?

"She decided to bear her cross alone."

"What a pity! Poor woman! Koffi, please don't push her to the wall..."

After a lengthy conversation that lasted for over one hour, I prayed for him and his family. Both of us wished each other good night, and he went upstairs to join his wife in bed.

Jumoke was still awake, and as soon as Koffi entered the room, she dropped her book and requested that they continue with the talk they started earlier in the kitchen. Koffi undressed but he was still wearing his Calvin Klein boxers. He did this on purpose, knowing fully well that his wife would be turned on erotically. He entered into the duvet and grabbed his wife, but she stopped him midway.

"Why are you doing this?" He asked ragingly.

With a soft voice, she said, "I want us to talk first. Yes, let's talk about us. You love having sex. This is typical of Ghanaian men."

"I beg your pardon! Are you saying Nigerian men don't like sex?"

"I'm not saying so."

"Okay! My baby girl, when are we starting the romantic talk?"

"We have started already. Koffi, you see, we are not in love like before. When we met, we felt a tremendous sense of passion for each other. Both of us were inseparable, and we couldn't keep our hands off each other. A few years into our marriage, things have changed. What's happening to us?" She asked while getting emotional.

"Nothing is happening to us."

"I'm afraid. We are drifting apart gradually."

"Don't be afraid, we will fix it."

"Fix what?"

"Our marriage. Our sex life. Our everything."

"First, try to fix your life. Your gambling. Your alcoholism. Your infidelity! Do you know that I find it really hard to yield myself to you sexually? I'm afraid of STDs or even HIV AIDS. Any married man patronising clubs or having side chicks is endangering his life and that of his wife..."

"But do you think I'm stupid? I use protection..."

"What type of protection?"

"Condom..."

"Condom?"

"Yes."

"But is condom hundred per cent safe?"

"I don't think so ... even deep inside me, I always felt guilty. You know, no condom can cover me from guilt."

"Hope you really know that... Koffi, what is so special about those girls, sexually?

"Like how?"

"Like the way you prefer them to me. Am I not satisfying you enough?"

"You are trying but..."

"But what?"

"Jumoke, you know I like blow jobs but after our wedding you became restrictive. I tried to persuade you but you refused to align with my sexual orientation or preference. You even became religious about it..."

"But Koffi, that shouldn't pull you away into the arms of those seductive girls."

"The fact is that most married men that have side chicks are not satisfied at home."

"What you are saying in essence is that you are not satisfied... But what can I do to satisfy you?

"You know what to do... But don't worry, my cousin has even talked sense into me. I had to open up to him."

"But you said I should not tell him..."

"I had to, especially when he was talking to me about the salvation of God, how he got saved and all that. Do you know that Pumaya's grandpa was the chief talisman of their village? When Pumaya was a little boy in the village, his old man was grooming him as his successor."

"Ahh, what a shame! So this fine young man would have ended up serving the devil."

"My baby, I think I'm a changed person now. I have promised God and Pumaya never to go back to my vomit again. I have turned a new leaf. I have changed for good..."

"Seriously?"

"I'm damn serious."

"That will be the greatest news of the century, but you have been a Church-goer all this while."

"Yes, but you know that going to church is different from a personal relationship with Christ. I have decided to take my life seriously."

"That's nice. Hope it will last ..."

"Yes, I believe it will, by God's grace!"

By this time, his hands were all over his wife's smooth and succulent body. No more resistance! Within a few minutes, she began to moan as he slipped into her wet and slippery tunnel of love. Then a few moments of silence, like the silence after a storm, the reconciled lovers laid back after being spent from vigorous lovemaking. Koffi's mind flashed back to when he first met Jumoke and the passion with which he was chasing after her in the University of Lagos campus. In a moment, his mind was racing to and fro, he managed to settle on the current romantic time out. He whispered to his wife, "My baby, I look forward to reinventing this again and again. Would you like it?"

"Yes."

Wrapped and cuddling in each other's arms, they slept soundly like Siamese twin babies.

CHAPTER

Six

After my visit to the Koffis, I rushed back to the hostel in order to honour Mr and Mrs Jasper Okoko's invitation to their house. The distance from YDI Centre to Mr Jasper Okoko's house was not all that far. I felt we could stroll to his house but my friend, Benson felt otherwise. To him, taking a motorcycle ride, popularly called Okada in Lagos would be better.

"It is better for us to 'fly' Okada!" Benson opined.

"Let's just stroll and exercise our bodies," I countered his opinion.

"Ahh, no no, the place is far. Okada is better. Are you afraid of Okada?"

"Not really. In Ghana, we use motorcycle taxis too. We use them to navigate through narrow roads, rough terrains, and remote areas..."

"Here in Lagos, we use them to meander through the hectic Lagos traffic... Do you realise that unemployment has driven many youths into Okada business to earn a living?"

"Yes."

"

"So let's help our youths by patronising Okada."

"Benson, don't be sentimental."

"I'm not sentimental. Our patronage will put money in their pockets."

"What about taxi cab drivers or even Uber drivers, they too need our patronage."

"I know you don't like Okada operators because they are prone to accidents."

"Yes. Okada operators drive too fast and recklessly. My friend, the risk involved is too high. Let's consider that."

"Many people don't really consider that. What they bother about is how to catch up with an appointment... Here in Lagos, I have seen businessmen, government workers, and students using motorcycle taxis to overcome terrific traffic congestion..."

"I don't like Lagos because of the chaotic traffic menace."

"Me, I like Lagos! I like the hustle and bustle of the city!"

"Ahh, let's go, we are getting late for the appointment," I urged.

We rushed out of the hostel and picked an Okada that just dropped off a fellow student. We agreed on a price and climbed the motorcycle like monkeys.

Within a few minutes from the hostel, it began to rain unannounced. Before we knew it, we were all drenched. As if that was not enough, the Okada operator in the course of avoiding a big stone, mistakenly drove us into a pull of dirty water and our clothes got stained. The operator began to plead, "I'm sorry. I'm really sorry. I didn't really know the stone would cause an accident."

"But you should have been more careful!..." I screamed, venting my anger.

"Sorry Sir. Sorry. It wasn't intentional...," the operator kept pleading.

Benson, being a tall and energetic young man, wanted to be physical with the Okada man, but I restrained him. I told him, "Benson, my friend, what are you trying to do? Fight? After all, we are not injured..."

"But he got our dresses stained."

"Don't worry."

Benson was really vexed, and his look showed he was mad inside. He started blaming himself, "Pumaya, it's all my fault. I accept the blame."

"Don't worry. It's not your fault. Did you cause the rain to fall? Did you cause the accident? I presume it was meant to happen."

"No. It's my fault. If I didn't urge you to use Okada, we wouldn't have had an accident or be drenched with rain..."

"Okada man, please take us back to the hostel. We just have to change our dresses," I instructed.

"Okay Sir."

The rain started to subside. We climbed the bike and the Okada operator rode gently back to the hostel. Some fellow students who saw us depart earlier began to sympathise with us. One of them asked: "What happened my people?"

"We fell into the muddy lgando river," Benson replied jokingly but sarcastically.

We all burst into laughter.

Within 10 minutes, we changed our clothes and off we went, riding on the bike again. By this time, the rain had totally abated. I pleaded with the Okada operator not to allow the affliction to happen the second time. Heeding to my plea, he became more cautious than before. He conveyed us gently and safely to our destination.

The access road to Mr Jasper Okoko's house was paved with Italian club stones, shaped octagonally like French avenues. The avenues were lined on both sides of the divide with royal palm trees and a beautifully manicured lushgreen lawn. The entrance gate was a remotely controlled sliding gate, having solar power as a backup power source, which moved noiselessly at a command from the remote control with the security guard.

As soon as we entered the beautiful premises, the security guard asked us to fill the visitor's form, which we did promptly. He called via the intercom to intimate Mrs Jasper that we had arrived. In a few minutes, a tall, slim looking lady came for us. She ushered us into the visitors living room and asked us to take our seats. We sat down.

I used my eyes to survey the living room. I whispered to Benson, "No doubt, this sofa seat is beautiful and expensive. Wow, look at the giant television screen on the wall. I think it is measuring over ten feet in diameter. This is a cinema house..."

Benson interrupted me, "That is hyperbolic. You are exaggerating, this is not a cinema house!"

"If the visitors' living room is this big and beautiful, what will you say about the family living room or their bedrooms? Nigeria is a rich country."

"I'm overwhelmed by the flooring," Benson opined.

"Yes, me too. This floor is made of sapphire coloured Italian marble, the best money can buy."

"Wow, truly, this house is beautiful. Just take a look at the POP design. The ceiling is stepped with beautiful architraves and conics to match."

"Yes, I can see that the conics have flowering petals and vines engraving all through the various levels and parameters of the ceiling."

"Can you see the light inside the ceiling?"

"Yes, they are all recessed, but for the pendant drop-down Chandelier."

As we were busy assessing the beauty of their home and discussing, Mrs Jasper Okoko appeared from an inner room and greeted us, "Good evening, Mr Abdulai Pumaya and Mr Egwu Benson, how are you guys doing?"

We quickly stood up and simultaneously replied, "Good evening Ma'am! We are doing fine. "

"You guys are welcome to our modest home."

"Thanks Ma," we responded.

Benson, the loquacious one, said, "Ma, this is not a modest home. This is a beautiful home"

"Thank you for the compliment, Benson."

"Thanks Ma."

"I know the rain must have made you guys to come late."

"Yes Ma. The rain delayed us," I responded.

"Ma, not only the rain. We had a minor Okada accident," Benson chipped in.

"Ahh, so sorry about that. Are you both okay?

"Yes, we are okay Ma," I replied.

"My husband too is held up in Lagos traffic. But he will soon be home."

"Okay Ma," we chorused.

"Please excuse me, I'm busy in the kitchen." She stepped out of our presence.

I challenged Benson, "Why are you so loquacious? Did you have to tell her about the motorbike accident? Wisdom demands that we be discreet about some things."

"Sorry."

"Okay."

After about 30 minutes, Mrs Okoko came to announce that her husband was back and that we should follow her to the dining room.

"Nice again to have you here."

"Thanks Ma. We appreciate your hospitality."

"Ahh! Pumaya and Benson, how are you guys doing?"

"We are doing fine Sir," Benson and I replied simultaneously.

"Please sit down," Mrs Okoko urged us. Turning to her teenage daughters who sat with their Dad on the glass dining table, she asked them to greet us. They did, but with mumbled words that we couldn't even understand.

The girls were unfriendly and unexcited as if their Mom had scolded them earlier. Mrs Okoko served her husband and asked us and her daughters to serve ourselves. Without further ado, I promptly served myself and started eating. "Ummm, Madam, this is tasty," I commended.

"Thank you."

"My pleasure, Madam."

"Pumaya, please feel free. Do you love our Nigerian cuisine?" Mr Okoko asked.

"Yes Sir. I love it. There is a Nigerian Restaurant in Accra where my Nigerian friend and I used to patronise."

"That's nice... Benson, what about you? Do you love Nigerian food."

"Yes Sir. I'm a Nigerian Sir."

"Oh! Yes, I remember. You are from Northern Nigeria."

"Yes Sir, I'm from North-Central, popularly known as Middle Belt, Sir."

"Yes, yes. The food basket of Nigeria!"

"Yes Sir."

An hour or so later, we moved to the family living room where Mr Jasper engaged us in a conversation.

"Pumaya, have you guys been enjoying your training?"

"Yes Sir. I love your course on Character Development Sir."

"What is the profound statement you remember from the course?"

"Charisma could take you to the top, but only character can sustain you at the top."

"Sir, as for me, I remember an incident in the class while you were teaching," Benson contributed.

"Which incident is that?" Mr Okoko interjected.

"Sir, while you were teaching on character, a student's phone rang with a funny ring tone. The student, Douglas Idoko, was acutely aware of his inability to turn off his phone anytime it rang. As he was trying fruitlessly to turn it off, the phone fell off his hands and scattered on the floor. He was sorry for the distraction his phone had caused, and for disrupting the flow of your lecture. We all thought you were going to be mad at him, but you turned the class into a bout of humour. You jokingly said, You and your phone lack character!"

"Yes, I remember that incident. We had many funny participants in your class."

"Sir, do you also remember Jerome Okplogidi, the guy with a funny-looking black suit?"

"Yes, I do remember his funny looks and funny dressing. He was the one who made a side comment that Idoko's phone was a China-made 'chinko' phone. And that it's only fake phones from China that will scatter like that ..."

"Sir, you told us a story about China that I will never forget for life," I chipped in.

"Which one is that?"

"Sir, it's a story about the Great China Wall."

"Ok. Retell the story now."

"The Chinese built their Great Wall believing that it would keep invaders at bay, because they thought it was impossible for anyone to scale it, given its insurmountable height. However, within the first century of the construction of the wall, the Chinese were invaded three times. Every time the invaders came, they had no need to climb over the wall; because each time they came, they were able to bribe the guards on duty at the gate, and the gate was opened for them. The Chinese took pains to build the wall but they forgot to build the character of the guards who were supposed to secure the walls...."

"The great lesson of the story is that character-building precedes wall-building," Benson interjected.

"Excellent! I'm very proud of you guys!"

"Sir, is a person of character born or made?"

"He or she is made, not born. Please understand that character supersedes charisma! Charisma truly can take you to the highest position in Ministry but only character or integrity will sustain you! Character is that part of you that is important to God. A wise man said, 'Reputation is what others think of us; character is what God knows of us.' Character is about self-discipline! A man of character is self-disciplined."

"Sir, your style of teaching is simple but powerful and highly illuminating."

"Thanks. Your graduation is around the corner."

"Yes Sir," we responded in unison.

"I wish you guys the best. Be a practitioner of all that you have learnt. Okay?"

"Okay Sir."

"My driver will drop you guys off in the hostel."

"Okay Sir. Thank you Sir."

"My pleasure."

CHAPTER
Seven

On our graduation day, I was in the hostel putting on my graduation gown and cap when a fellow graduand beckoned on me that a lady was looking for me. I was wondering who the lady might be. On a second thought, I guessed it could be Jumoke, as she had called me earlier that they might come early for my graduation.

Immediately, I dashed downstairs to see the lady looking for me. Yes, my guess was accurate. It was Jumoke! I greeted her excitedly: "Hi, Jumoke. Good morning!"

"Pumaya! Good morning. Congratulations on your graduation."

"My pleasure! Thank you for coming to celebrate with me. What about Koffi and the kids?"

"They went to another event. We had a scheduled event which required our participation, but I chose to attend yours instead."

"Ahh, that's nice of you. Thank you for coming all the way from Lekki. I appreciate your sacrifice."

"I appreciate you more. You don't know what your coming to our home has done."

"How do you mean?" I asked inquisitively.

She drew close to me and said, "Your cousin has changed for good! He said you converted him."

"Ahh! No, I don't have the power to convert a soul but God does. We preach and God converts! Who am I but a vessel in His hands."

"For over two weeks, Koffi has not gone out to clubs or drank alcohol. Pumaya! That's a miracle!"

"We give God all the glory..."

"Amen."

"Please come with me, and let me show you where to sit. You know, you are my special guest, as such, you have a special seat. Let's go..."

"Okay! I like this place. It's so beautiful and clean."

"Yes, YDI Centre is a paragon of beauty."

The graduation ceremony was very brief. Within one hour, the whole event was over. Jumoke was impressed with the brevity of the ceremony. And she made it known to me, "I love this Ministry, they are good with time management."

"Yes, time management is one of the core courses we were taught. Our chief trainer, Mr Jasper Okoko does not tolerate mismanagement of time or resources."

"Other Ministries will waste time unnecessarily."

"Please let's go towards the garden to take some pictures and have refreshments," I urged her.

"No, I won't wait for refreshments. I have to rush and pick up Koffi and the kids. It was nice that your event was brief. I brought you a cooler of fried rice and some drinks to share with your friends. I have a token of 100 thousand Naira for you. Please, it's small, just manage it..."

"Wow! This is too much! Thanks so much... May God reward you immensely."

"Amen! Amen!"

"Let's take some snapshots before you go."

"Okay."

"Thank you."

Jumoke and I posed for some shots, and I saw her off to her red Toyota SUV with tinted glasses. While seated in

her posh vehicle, with the engine still idling, she asked
me: "When are you going back to Ghana?"

"Tomorrow."

"Do you know that nations are closing down their
airports due to the Coronavirus pandemic?"

"No. I'm just hearing this."

"Land borders are getting closed too. But I don't know
about West African land borders."

"Wow! Please, my best wishes to Koffi and kids... I have
to book my flight right now."

"Yes! That's a nice move. Best of luck. My warmest
regards to your wife..."

"Thanks for everything."

Quickly, I went to the Garden area of the Centre and
took some pictures with my course mates who were still
milling around the premises enjoying the happy moment.
I removed my academic gown and headed for the hostel
with great anxiety. In a jiffy, I booked a flight ticket
online with Arik Airline for 3 p.m. that afternoon.

A few hours later, I made it to the airport. There were
many passengers like me trying frantically to beat the
lockdown. At the Arik airline check-in desk, I was told

that my ECOWAS ID which I had used earlier to book my ticket was not acceptable, and that only International passport holders could travel. I begged them to do me a favour but to no avail. My next step was to demand a ticket refund. I turned to one of the airline staff and asked, "Madam, I want my refund. How do I go about it?"

"Sorry that we couldn't help you... Heh, you have to go to our Head Office and lodge a formal complaint. Customer service staffers should be able to tell you what to do. Okay?"

"Okay."

"But know that it might take one or two months to effect a refund."

"Why?"

"I don't know."

Leaving the airport in a hurry, I returned to YDI Centre, where I had lodged all through the Training programme.

The following day, 28th March 2020, Lagos State government announced a total lockdown due to the COVID-19 pandemic. In a state of confusion and frustration, I went to see Mr Jasper Okoko for counsel, and he advised me to maintain calmness.

Calmness? My mind started running riot with many conflicting thoughts and all manner of questions. Where would I stay now that the training was over? Would the training centre management allow me to stay in the hostel? How long would the lockdown take? How would my wife manage without me if the lockdown was for a long haul? What about my wife's pregnancy?

The management of the Centre offered me accommodation at the Mission Lodge. This offer brought me appreciable relief. Although the Mission Lodge was not as comfortable as I thought, I was eminently enthralled. After all, during our MPC training, Mr Jasper Okoko, the Chief Trainer, had prepared us for a tough life. He used to say in his lectures, "... soldiers are not groomed in Sheraton hotels but in the bush. As such, soldiers of the Lord must be prepared for uncomfortable situations always."

I met Benson Egwu and Adakole Oha in the three-bedroom apartment all ensuite. My room was close to the entrance door; that meant that I was like a gatekeeper to the apartment. Upon my arrival, three of us discussed and agreed on how to operate and live together in harmony. Benson volunteered to be our chief chef. The young bachelor loved cooking. And he also loved eating what he cooked. He could win an eating contest. Adakole and I usually enjoyed his tasty food and we were very magnanimous with compliments. Benson could go to any extent for anyone who cared to compliment him.

After dinner, while in a relaxed mood, we sat down chatting and discussing the lockdown.

"What's your view about this Coronavirus pandemic lockdown?" I asked Adakole.

"My view is that our government is not doing enough to educate the people about the Coronavirus pandemic."

"Why do you think the government is not doing much?"

"They should be more proactive. To me, it shouldn't be all about shutting down the country..."

"Don't mind our government officials, they are out to siphon money from the national treasury in the name of fighting the virus..."

"Benson, it's a shame that you Nigerians don't trust your government," I interrupted him.

"What about Ghanaians, do you trust your own government?" He fired back with a question.

"My friend, it is an African problem. Many nations in Africa are yet to be blessed with leadership that is trustworthy and corruption-free. Truly, the good and beautiful leaders are not yet born..."

"That reminds me of a great novel, 'The Beautiful Ones are not yet Born' written by a Ghanaian novelist, Ayi Kwei Armah in the sixties. Have you read the novel?" Benson asked.

"No. I have not. But I have heard about it... But Benson, why are you so critical about your government?"

"I'm not a government antagonist. But I dislike to the utmost any government that tells lies with reckless abandon or governs the people via propaganda," He replied.

Adakole chipped in: "Our government is heavily corrupt! Pumaya, does Ghana have problem with corruption?"

"Yes of course, but not endemically pronounced like Nigeria."

"Are you saying Nigeria's case is irredeemable?"

"I'm not saying so. I'm only saying that Ghana's case is not as terrible as Nigeria's. Corruption is an African virus!"

"No! Corruption is a global problem just like Coronavirus. The Western world is a great custodian of corruption. See how African leaders steal their nations' wealth and siphon billions for safekeeping in Western banks."

"My brother, I agree with you. If our stolen wealth or money is repatriated today, Western banks will collapse, hence their unwillingness to agree to repatriation."

"Corruption is even more deadly than Coro!"

The three of us started laughing.

My phone rang and I picked it, saying, "Hello, hello, hello," and dashed into my room to answer the call in privacy.

It was my wife who called again. Her call has been very regular recently. She had been very worried about me. As such, she would always call to find out how I was faring and also to discuss her emotional and physiological state. With a loving tone, I said, "Honey, what's up? Hope you're doing good. Are you fine?"

"Fine."

"How are you doing?"

"Fine."

"Please tell me, are you okay?"

"I said I'm fine! I'm okay!"

"But you don't sound happy like the last time we spoke."

"I'm getting tired!" She muttered."I'm getting bothered! When will all this end? I find myself crying every night!" She started crying. And I had to do a lot of consoling but I controlled my emotion as a strong man.

"Please stop crying! We are going to overcome this challenge for sure."

She cried out louder and louder! I could no longer hold myself, I too burst into tears. Benson and Adakole ran from the dining area to my room. They were perplexed, not knowing what to do. They tried to console me, but I refused to be consoled as I cried out some more.

Benson asked me if he could be allowed to talk with my wife. I gave him the phone but my wife had hung up. Adakole queried Benson, "Are you married? What do you know about husband and wife matter? A bloody bachelor like you..."

Benson got offended and started lambasting Adakole for his intrusion into his bachelorhood.

He told him in clear terms that he was not pleased.

He said, "I'm better off than you. I'm in a serious relationship with a pretty lady. You? No lady yet! You are still searching. After all, I don't have to be married to counsel married people. Mr Jasper Okoko used to say that, 'information is superior to experience.' I have veritable information about harmony and bliss in marriage.”

 “Sorry my brother, I didn't mean to hurt you,” Adakole apologised.

“Okay... Apology accepted.”

“You have challenged me today. After the lockdown, I will go get my own lady...”

“That will be nice. You are not growing younger, but older. Do you want to marry at forty-something? Don't you want to see your children's children?”

“Ummm, I want to...”

Three weeks later, there was a knock at the door. I rushed to open the door, and a lanky young man with a funny look and smile entered our living room. With a look of surprise, I opened my mouth wide and screamed: “MC Touchnot! Where are you coming from and where are you going? Why are you not observing the lockdown rule? Surprised to see you.”

“I'm more surprised than you, good to see you again,” MC Touchnot, the budding comedian responded.

Adakole queried the comedian while laughing, “My guy, where are your hand gloves and face-mask? We are observing the lockdown rules here. Let me give you a hand sanitiser.”

He dashed to a corner and pulled a bottle of sanitiser from a cupboard near the visitor's restroom, and administered it to our hungry-looking guest.

"Thank you for fumigating my hands," MC Touchnot said, humorously.

"It is not fumigation!"

"Okay, it is sanitisation, eh?

"More like it."

"My guys, you are shocked to see me here, eh?"

"Yes! But how did you escape or dodge those security officers?" Benson asked.

"You know hunger can make a hungry man jump the tallest fence. Na hunger make me jump here. I learnt you guys have enough food here... I finished mine during the first 14 days of the lockdown!"

"Really?"

"Yes oh, my friend Benson. Let me soak garri with groundnut. I have been trekking from Igando to this place. Thank God I made it without fainting on the way..."

Benson, the chief chef of our apartment dashed into the kitchen and prepared hot eba for MC Touchnot, which he ate with relish. After the meal, he told us that he was prepared to become a soldier so as to have some food to eat, as there was no lack of food in the officers' lodge.

"MC Touchnot, when are you going back to your place?" Adakole asked.

"Ahh, maybe after the lockdown..."

"No problem. You can stay as long as you want. Okay?"

"Thank you, my Ghanaian friend."

One fateful evening, four of us felt we needed to stretch our legs by taking a stroll. And within 30 minutes of strolling in the vicinity, some law enforcement officers accosted us and bundled us into their pickup van. We pleaded with them but to no avail. One of the officers took Benson aside to a corner and advised him to give them bribe so that we could be left off the hook. Benson told him: "We are Missionaries, we don't give bribes..."

The pot-bellied officer replied, "When you get to our station, you will see hell..."

"Sir, please have mercy on us. We don't want to go to your station!"

"Do you know about Matthew 5:25?"

"No Sir."

"And you call yourself a Missionary. That scripture is saying that you should always agree with officers on the way. You better settle with us quickly if not we will throw you guys into the cell, and you will experience hell. Our cell is hell," the officer threatened.

CHAPTER
Eight

A few hours later, the pot-bellied officer made good his promise by bringing us to their station. As if that was not enough, they gave us the first harsh treatment by commanding us to remove our shoes and to sit down on a bare floor outside. Without hesitation or complaining, we quickly complied with their instruction. My heart began to palpitate speedily, as I had never been arrested or brought to any police station in my life; and the reality of being arrested and brought to a police station in a foreign land brought tears into my eyes. I became intensely emotional.

The Divisional Crime Officer, Mr Acheme, a gentle but serious-looking officer, came out of his office and inquired from one of his junior officers.

"Who are those hoodlums? Are they part of the criminal gang harassing Lagos during this lockdown?"

"No Sir."

"What's their crime?"

"Loitering Sir."

"Loitering during a lockdown? Go and handcuff them..."

"Yes Sir, but we don't have enough handcuffs, Sir."

"Okay. It's true, the criminal gang, popularly known as '1Million Boys' have exhausted our handcuffs."

The same pot-bellied officer came again and threatened us that he was going to charge us with those daredevil criminals for loitering and disturbing public peace during a lockdown. But MC Touchnot challenged him, "But you can't charge us with them. We are not... we are not criminals."

"You are criminals..."

"We are not Sir!"

"Young man, you want to teach me my job ehh? I have been doing this job for over 27 years. You better shut up your mouth or I'll shut it for you."

The front desk constables rushed at MC Touchnot and started slapping and ill-treating him for daring to challenge their superior officer.

Inspector Olodi instructed his men to throw us into one of the cells where hardened criminals were kept. "When those criminals deal with you, you will never open your dirty and smelling mouth to challenge an officer of the law," he said sarcastically.

As soon as we got into the cell, the criminals rushed at us like hungry wolves. We received our first baptism of fire that started with beating as was predicted by the officer. No doubt, the beating was merciless and extreme; I even fainted as a result of it, and I had to be rushed to the police clinic within the station.

Within an hour, Uncle Emeka arrived the police station and went straight to the front desk to inquire about us. He was told that we were in the cell. He offered to bail us but he was unsuccessful. He was still talking with the front desk junior officers when the Divisional Crime Officer came in. Emeka recognised him. He too knew Emeka, as both of them had served in a Joint Ministerial Task Force a few years back. Both greeted each other warmly.

"Oga Emeka! What are you doing here?" The Crime Officer, Mr Acheme asked.

"Let's go to your office," Emeka requested.

They stepped out of the open office and went to Mr Acheme's office.

"Oga sit down Sir. You are welcome Sir! What's the matter Sir?"

"My in-law told me that some of his young men were arrested and brought to your station," Emeka replied.

"Yes Sir, they were brought here a few hours ago. It's a case of loitering Sir. They broke the lockdown emergency law Sir."

"Why? Don't they know about the lockdown?"

"I don't know for them Sir."

"Please do me a favour and help me release them."

"It's hard Sir. Even one of them was challenging my officer, but let me see what I can do for an old friend. Who knows tomorrow? I may need your help too tomorrow. What goes around comes around Sir."

An officer was mandated to bring us out. But he brought only three, Benson, Adakole and MC Touchnot.

Mr Acheme asked, "What about the fourth person?"

"In the clinic Sir."

"In the clinic? What happened to him?"

"The criminals in the cell, Sir, he is a very fragile young man Sir. He couldn't withstand their bashing."

"But they are not criminals. Why take them to the hardened criminals' cell in the first place?"

"Sir, it's Officer Olodi that commanded us to deal with them Sir."

"Tell Inspector Olodi to see me later!" The DCO
instructed. He turned to Emeka and said, "We have so
many overzealous officers in the Force, and they do
whatever they want..."

Meanwhile, my friends were looking so beaten,
humiliated and agitated. Emeka was angry with them,
and he showed it by the way he reprimanded them,
"Why were you people loitering? Didn't you know about
the lockdown?"

"We knew Sir... We are sorry Sir."

"Sorry for yourselves!"

Emeka and his DCO friend came to the clinic to see how
I was faring. My condition had stabilised greatly and the
doctor decided to free me. Without much hassles, after
fulfilling the conditions for our bail, we were released.

On our way, Uncle Emeka gave us a proper lecture about
the lockdown and why we must obey the laws. He
started his lecturing: "A lockdown is a security measure
taken during a critical crisis to prevent people from
leaving or entering states or nations. Our government put
this measure in place to slow the spread of this deadly
Coronavirus. It is for your good. You must obey the
law..."

Still looking petrified and hurting from the beating, I appreciated him: "Thank you Sir, we are grateful Sir. If not for you, we would have slept in the police cell. You are my angel, Sir. I had a dream that depicted this incident."

"Wow, are you Joseph the dreamer?"

"No Sir."

"Sorry about the beating. Thank God, you didn't die. Fainting is a step away from death you know?"

"Sir, those criminals were wicked to me. They were raining blows on me, as if I was their sworn enemy."

Uncle Emeka advised us, "Please, do not loiter again!"

"Sir, we were not actually loitering. We only took a stroll around our vicinity Sir," MC Touchnot responded.

"In a lockdown, you are meant to stay inside your house. Nothing like strolling. Okay?"

"Okay Sir!"

He dropped us close to the mission lodge and drove off.

No doubt, we were famished. We needed food badly but the first thing we did when we got home was to have our bath, as we were smelling like rotten eggs. No one would go into a police cell and come out smelling fresh. No. Not at all! Benson quickly warmed the rice he had cooked earlier in the day, and he was so kind as to serve us. We all ate. And we retired to our rooms.

Around midnight, David Ehikowoicho, a friend of mine, called: "Hello, Pumaya. What's up with you?"

"I'm okay. And you?"

"I'm okay too."

"I learnt you're still in Lagos."

"Yes. The lockdown affected my journey back to Ghana."

"Oh, you are facing restrictions."

"Yes, my friend."

"It's terrible here too. Hope you are in touch with people in Ghana?"

"Yes ooo! They too are facing the effects of the lockdown big time."

"It's a global problem..."

"Here in Lagos, the government kept urging us to stay indoors and to maintain social distancing."

"Yes, that's good. Here in New York, social distancing has become a new normal..."

"But can there be social distancing in places like Lagos slums?"

"Some parts of New York are like Lagos slums. President Donald Trump has declared a national emergency as cases and deaths in the United States skyrocketed. Just recently, a top New York City doctor, one Dr Lorna Breen, who was on the front line of the US fight against Coronavirus took her own life."

"What a pity! I pity America, almighty America."

"My friend, there is nothing almighty about America, especially concerning the handling of this deadly virus. Have you not heard that the high and mighty in politics, sports and entertainment have been grounded?"

"Yes. There is a suspension of some air and ground travels. Schools are closed. Churches are closed..."

"My dear, you know Americans love eating out. No more luxury of eating in restaurants for now."

"Lagos is a tough city."

"New York is tougher."

"Do you know that I'm just returning from the police station?"

"Ahh! What happened?"

"The police arrested me and my apartment mates."

"Why? What did you guys do?"

"Nothing! But they said that we contravened the law guiding the lockdown. The task force saw us on the street and picked us up to their station."

"Just like that?"

"Yes, just like that."

"Hope you guys were not manhandled or molested?"

"My Oh my! We were beaten to stupor, not by the police though."

"Who beat you guys?"

"Criminals! We were thrown into the cell where hardened criminals were kept..."

"Bullshit! But do the policemen have the right to do that?

"No! One of the officers did that just to punish us for our refusal to bribe them. He even wrongly quoted Matthew 5:25 to validate his bribe-taking..."

"What a pity! Nigerian policemen can do anything to collect bribe... Pumaya, what's happening there? I can hear sounds like gunshots."

"My dear, you are right."

"Are you safe?"

"Yes. But virtually every night some bad boys go from street to street, and house to house, molesting and robbing people."

"What? That's unacceptable. What about security personnel?"

"They are not available around here."

"What a pity! You guys are at the mercy of those robbers."

"No! We are at the mercy of God."

"Ummm, that's true."

"The security challenge here in Lagos is enormous. Every day, I live in fear. I can't wait to return to Ghana."

"Yes oh. Security is better in Ghana."

"Yes. By far."

There were more deafening gunshots. It was as if we were in a war front. I quickly cut off my conversation with David. I then beckoned on my apartment mates to join me in prayers for God's mercy and protection. Before we commenced our prayers, I charged them with few words: "Beloved friends, we must trust God to keep us in safety. No doubt, we are in perilous or difficult times. Truly, we are in such a time when many people's hearts are failing them. But our case is different! Let us not plunge into fear..."

There were more gunshots. We overheard the boys demanding for food in the six-block of flats next to ours. They commanded, "Bring out your food. We are hungry. If you give us food, we will not hurt you. But if you refuse to give us, you will be killed..."

Adakole jumped up and was pacing up and down like a frightened puppy.

 "Let's pray, let's pray. I want to go into my room," he said in a panicky voice.

"My friend you are panicking. You don't have to."

"I'm not panicking. Let's pray."

"No, let me conclude my sharing first."

Benson calmed Adakole. But he was still agitated.

I continued, "No evil will come near this apartment. I assure you. It is the Lord that watches over us like the mother hen. Benson, please could you quickly pray for us?"

"Yes, let's pray. In Jesus name, oh God send your angels to take charge over us now. Father, keep us safe from the bad boys out there. Father, secure us and keep us in safety via your angelic protection. I invoke the power in the name of Jesus Christ for our safety tonight..."

Adakole and I responded, "Amen." Before Benson could wrap up his prayers, Adakole rushed into his room and locked his door, still in fright, trembling like a leaf driven by the wind..

He did not even say, 'good night' to us.

CHAPTER
Nine

In the morning, we were extremely happy and thankful to God for surviving the shooting ordeal in the night. Even though, we were not directly affected, yet, with a heart of empathy, we were moved by the crying and wailing of our neighbours. Personally, I was touched in no small measure. For the first time, we were beginning to be bothered about our safety in Alakuko. Adakole suggested that Mr Jasper Okoko, our benefactor should be briefed; a suggestion we all resonated with. I was mandated to interface with him. Immediately, I called and narrated to him about the security challenge at Alakuko community. And he promised to intervene.

A few minutes later, Mr Okoko was pacing up and down in his living room as he was disturbed about our safety. He breathed deeply and stood. He lifted his left hand to his brow. His pretty wife came downstairs, looked at him and said, "You're looking worried, hope all is well."

He sat on a soft sofa and crossed his legs. Mrs Okoko came close and sat beside him.

"What's happening? Anything?"

"Nothing much."

"Are you okay?"

"I'm okay. But this lockdown is getting on my nerves..."

"Anything else?" His wife asked.

"I got a call from the mission lodge half an hour ago that saddens me."

"Ahh, hope the young men are okay... any problem with them again?"

"They said their lives are now in danger as there was shooting in their area yesterday night. Pumaya told me that they could not sleep."

"Oh, I feel for them."

"My dear, I'm beginning to feel so traumatised and frustrated about this lockdown."

"Ummm, you just have to encourage yourself. Let's keep praying about this storm, and I know for sure, God will soon stop it...What about Pumaya and his friends?"

"Oh yes, that reminds me. Let me call your brother, he should know what to do."

"Yes, he might make some useful contacts in the police high command. The security of Alakuko community must be beefed up."

"Let me call him."

Mr Jasper Okoko picked his cellular phone and called Uncle Emeka.

"Hello... hello, Emeka. Good morning."

"Good morning Sir."

"What about your children, especially your little rascal?"

"They are doing fine Sir. What about my sister?"

"She too is doing fine."

"And the girls?"

"They are fine! You know them. They are in the kitchen preparing breakfast."

"Okay Sir."

"I got an SOS from Alakuko a while ago."

"What is it about Sir?"

"The security challenge over there is deteriorating so badly, to the extent that my young men could not sleep at night due to constant intrusion into the community by armed gangs."

"I'm not surprised Sir. The crime rate has even jumped up during the lockdown."

"Emeka, what can you do for the community?"

"Sir, I will talk with the Lagos State Commissioner of Police. He will do something about it. Don't worry Sir! The problem will be fixed."

"Ummm, thank you very much for your support always."

"My pleasure Sir. I will be at your place in the evening Sir."

"Okay, that will be nice... Till you come."

"Yes Sir."

Mr Jasper Okoko's pretty daughters were done with cooking and setting the table for breakfast. On the table, there were assorted foods such as fried plantain, boiled yam, boiled eggs, fried eggs, milk, coffee, green tea, oatmeal and slices of bread. To the Okokos, breakfast was the most important meal of the day; as such, they took great deal of time to eat breakfast well. It was a family tradition or culture to eat breakfast within two or three hours after waking up. Mrs Okoko, a good cook and nutritionist had drummed it into the subconscious mind of her family members that breakfast was better for their metabolism. The only time the family did not have their breakfast was when they were engaged in the spiritual exercise of fasting.

Later in the evening, Emeka drove into the spacious compound on a visit, as he had promised earlier. Okoko's two teenage daughters ran out from their room to welcome their personable uncle who had been very supportive to them.

"Uncle Emeka, good evening Sir," they greeted in unison.

"Yes, good evening my pretty angels. Jessica, please give me a malt drink."

"Sir, what about your usual drink, I mean the fruit wine?"

"Oh, okay, bring it with a chilled bottle of water."

"Okay Sir. But uncle, chilled water is not good for your health."

"Doctor the doctor, my doctor, allow me to take this one today. Sun has been beating me since afternoon. I need something cold to cool my head."

In a moment, Jessica brought a bottle of non-alcoholic wine and water. But as she was about placing the wine on the side table, a beautiful china tumbler fell off her hand and broke. Immediately, she felt sorry for herself and said, "Uncle I'm sorry."

"Don't worry. Just go and get another one... Mary! Mary, bring broom and sweep this place."

"But uncle, I'm not the one who broke it. Let the person who broke the glass clean up the mess by herself. I don't know why she's always 'shaky -shaky' up and down..."

Emeka angrily yelled at Mary: "Stop that nonsense! Don't talk about your elder sister like that! Mary, stop your rudeness now! Come and clean up this place now or I will deal with you militarily!"

Grudgingly and tearfully, Mary picked a bunch of brooms and swept off the particles of broken glass.

"Ehh, Mary, thank you, my beloved angel. Be a good girl always. Okay?"

"Okay Sir."

"Give me a smile my dear."

"But uncle you like to shout at me. And I don't like it."

"I'm sorry. As a paramilitary officer, I have the proclivity to shout."

A few minutes later, Mr Okoko came downstairs. Emeka stood up to acknowledge his presence and he greeted his in-law, "Good evening Sir."

"Good evening. I overheard you shouting as usual. What is the matter?"

"Sir, it is Mary. I was reprimanding her."

"What did she do this time? That girl needs proper handling."

"She was rude to Jessica. Both of them are like cat and mouse."

"Yes! But why can't they just live amicably without fighting or quarrelling with each other?"

"Sir, they are teens and such misdemeanour will be expected from them."

Mr Jasper adjusted his eyeglasses and said, "Let's leave their matter alone and talk about more important issues. So how far with my request?"

"Everything is under wrap Sir. The Police Commissioner promised to send a detachment of Mobile Police Force to Alakuko community tonight Sir."

"Wow, that's a big relief for my people and the entire community."

"Yes Sir."

"Thank you so much Emeka. I'm most grateful!"

"My greatest pleasure Sir."

"Do you know that there had been a lot of outcry over the Coronavirus crisis?" Mr Okoko asked.

"I know Sir. These days, no day passes without us hearing one depressing news or the other."

"The most painful part is that social media has been awash with so many fake news. Have you heard about the conspiracy theories surrounding the Coronavirus?"

"Not really Sir."

"You mean... you have not heard about the conspiracy theories..."

"I have heard Sir. But I don't understand what some people are talking about Sir."

"Some so-called experts are saying that the Coronavirus was produced as a biological weapon in a laboratory in China and that the virus is spread by 5G wireless technology."

"Sir, I also heard that billionaire philanthropist Bill Gates created the virus in connivance with Chinese scientists in order to make more money."

Mr Okoko requested for a glass to share a drink with Emeka. "Personally, I don't believe that trash. But these days, many people are accusing him because he was insisting that the world population must be vaccinated before the world could return to normal."

"But Sir, is he God? Why must he talk with an air of pride and finality? I think he has personal or business interest."

"I don't think so..."

"I think so Sir."

"Did you know that he contributed millions of dollars to roll out polio from Nigeria?"

"I know Sir."

"We have to follow facts, I mean scientific facts, instead of conspiracy theories. Do you know that even in advanced countries, these conspiracies have had real-life consequences?"

"Like how, Sir?"

"Recently, I read about some people in Britain and Netherlands attacking and damaging radio towers, assumed to be carrying 5G technology."

"If such attacks are happening abroad, then much more attacks will happen in Nigeria."

"I agree with you completely."

"But Sir, why didn't people complain about 3G or 4G?"

"That's just the problem with conspiracy theories. Some people just sit in their homes or offices to write on issues they don't even have ideas about."

"Very unfortunate Sir."

"Very unfortunate indeed. Personal or group gain is behind most conspiracy theories."

"Yes Sir!"

"There was a film that was recently removed from YouTube for featuring fabricated claims about   Covid-19."

"Wow, that's nice!"

"But before they removed the video, over seven million people had viewed it. And this shows how popular and widely accepted conspiracy theories can be."

"Sir, thank you for educating me."

"My pleasure always."

"I want to be on my way Sir." Uncle Emeka stood up to go but Mr Okoko pleaded with him: "Please before you go, let me share with you a Coronavirus joke. During this lockdown, it is good to keep ourselves entertained especially with good comedy. Let me read this to your hearing. The title is, Coronavirus Revenge."

"An American, a German and a Chinese were arrested consuming alcohol which is a severe offence in Saudi Arabia. So for the terrible crime, they were each sentenced to 20 lashes of the whip.

As they were preparing for their punishment, the Sheik announced: "It's my first wife's birthday today, and she has asked me to allow each of you to make one wish before your whipping."

The German was first in line, he thought for a while and then said: "Please tie a pillow to my back." This was done, but the pillow only lasted 10 lashes as the whip tore through the pillow into his body and he had to be carried away bleeding and crying in pain. The Chinese was next. After watching the German in horror he said smugly: "Please fix two pillows to my back." But even two pillows could only take 15 lashes and the Chinese was also led away whimpering loudly.

The American was the last one up, but before he could say anything, the Sheik turned to him and said: "I like you Americans. For this, you may have two wishes!"

"Thank you, your Most Royal and Merciful highness," the American replied. "In recognition of your kindness, my first wish is that you give me not 20, but 100 lashes." With an admiring look on his face, the Sheik said unto the American, "Not only are you an honourable, handsome and powerful man, you are also very brave. If

100 lashes are what you desire, then so be it. And what is your second wish?" The Sheik asked. The American smiled and said, "Tie the Chinese to my back!"

"This is a beautiful joke!"

"Yes! It is!"

Both Mr Okoko and Uncle Emeka laughed so loudly that the people in the neighbourhood heard them.

CHAPTER

Ten

Early in the morning the following day, policemen invaded Alakuko community, harassing and molesting any youth they saw. Any rough-looking youth became a natural suspect to them.

Adakole informed us of his intention to step out to buy some stuff within our vicinity, but I dissuaded him from going out. I reminded him about how he was panicking the previous night due to the security challenge. I also told him about the ugly incident we had with the police. I emphatically told him, "Adakole, policemen are everywhere within this community. Let's be careful. The incident with the police has taught me a big lesson that some policemen are not friendly at all..."

Benson interjected, "Yes, it's true. Police brutality or oppression against innocent people is another global pandemic..."

"Benson, I'm in tandem with you... I agree with you completely. It's so fresh in my memory, how George

Floyd, a 46-year-old black man was killed by the police
outside a shop in Minneapolis, Minnesota."

"But the police are meant to protect lives, " Adakole
noted.

"That's the irony of life," I responded.

Adakole continued to express his view: "What a shame!
The police officer that killed the guy in the US was evil
and vicious."

"Yes, he was. The white police officer, Derek Chauvin,
knelt on Mr Floyd's neck while he was pinned to the
floor."

"That's wickedness of the highest order. We even have
worst cases in Nigeria," Benson quickly corroborated.

 "My friend, such cases don't happen only in Nigeria. It
happens all over Africa," I responded thoughtfully.

"Pumaya, the Police Force needs serious orientation and
constant re-orientation, " Adakole opined.

"Yes for sure!"

"Do you know that Mr Floyd said more than 20 times
that he could not breathe as he was restrained by the
officers?" Benson asked. "…And they did not listen or
care about his pleas. That is the wickedness of man.
Man's inhumanity to man."

"I won't go anywhere now until the coast is clear," Adakole declared.

I excused myself and went into my room to do some reading. And as I was about reading an interesting novel, a call came to distract me. Ahh, it was a bosom friend of mine named Dayo, a Logistics expert based in Paris, France.

"Hello, hello..." I said.

"Yes, hello."

Speaking with a voice depicting much concern, he asked me, "Pumaya, how are you coping in Lagos?"

"Good morning," I greeted.

"Sorry, good morning, I should have greeted you first. Pardon my poor manners."

"No problem. How are you doing?"

"I'm doing good... I heard you are stranded in Nigeria."

"Yes, Dayo, my friend. You can't believe it, the day I was to travel back to Ghana was the same day the Lagos State Government announced the lockdown. I bought Arik Airline ticket to fly out of Lagos but to no avail."

"Wow, poor you! I know you must have been frustrated and downcast."

"Yes of course. I'm all alone here in Lagos, facing all the challenges of the lockdown..."

"I can understand your plight. Are you in touch with your people in Ghana? Are they calling you?"

"Yes. I receive calls and WhatsApp messages from them regularly. But it's not like being there physically to enjoy their company."

"I can understand. You must have run out of money."

"Yes. But I thank God for His provisions. Some relatives and friends have been supportive financially. And even Mrs Jasper Okoko and her husband have been supplying food to us regularly."

"That's nice. I will send you my token too."

"Wow, that sounds great. Thank you in anticipation!"

"My pleasure. Hope you don't mind... let's use Zoom if you have the Apps on your phone."

"Yes, I have Zoom Apps on my iPad."

"That's great. Let's have a Zoom meeting so I can see your good-looking face."

"Hahaha! I like to see your face too."

Within a few seconds, he sent me his Zoom ID and code. And without shilly-shallying, I got connected.

"Ahh, Pumaya, I'm pleased to see your face!"

"Same here, Dayo! I'm excited to see you. You're looking so fresh."

"Thank you. Pumaya, but you are not looking your handsome, true self. You're looking so stressed. What's going on?"

"Ummm, you know the lockdown is getting stressful too. The fact that I'm in a foreign country makes my case precarious and depressing."

"I can understand. Sorry about that. But you just have to encourage yourself. It's a tough time..."

I promptly interjected, "Tough times never last but tough people do!"

"That's Robert Schuller's bestselling book, published in 1983!"

"Yes, yes. Dayo, I do remember. I read the book cover to cover many times. A highly motivational masterpiece!"

"I learnt many things from the man. He was the one who said, If you can dream it, you can do it!"

"In this season, we need a lot of motivational materials to motivate us not to give in to fears or challenges..."

"That's the spirit, my friend! Get tough. Be strong! Don't be stressed or depressed. The storm will soon be over!"

"Yes, I believe... but I'm getting so worried about the negative impact of the lockdown on us."

"But what can we do? It's a trying moment for the world."

"Yes. We have never seen this before."

"Not at all."

"I'm bothered and worried about our young people's education..."

"Yes. The truth is that many students have been significantly impacted by the lockdown," Dayo responded.

"I agree with you. The disruption is palpable and felt by many schools and institutions across Nigeria and Ghana."

"This new normal is that teaching and learning are moving online. This is unprecedented! Even assessments have also become digital."

"But in many African countries where there is weak infrastructure, learning will not take place at all. This means that students will lose 3-6 months of learning..."

"In Uganda, according to Dr Ruth Mirambe, a friend of mine, the lockdown has caused a lot of uncertainties regarding how the future will be in terms of progression in schools. She told me that in Uganda, only very few universities resorted to Online lectures which also proved futile as most students couldn't afford data bundles to access the Online programmes while some students are coming from deep down interior villages where there's poor or no network at all..."

"Africa, Oh my Africa! Why must we be facing all kinds of challenges like this? What's really wrong with Africa?"

"This problem is not an African problem. It is a global problem."

"But Africa needs to buckle up fast. In terms of technology, we have been left behind."

"Yemi, a lecturer friend of mine in the USA told me that Online teaching feels different. He loved making eye contact and seeing body languages of students when teaching. He also loved interacting physically not digitally with students."

"I can understand! We are having Zoom meeting now, looking at ourselves on iPad or phone screens... No doubt, physical interaction is superior to digital interaction."

"Yes, yes my friend."

"Yemi is a Science lecturer, do you think he could perform chemical reactions over the Internet?"

"Not at all!"

"How are you faring in Paris?"

"I'm faring well to a large extent."

"But is the lockdown not taking its toll on you?"

"Not really. I work from home majorly."

"Thank God you still have a job."

"Yes, I'm grateful. Many people are losing their jobs daily. The unemployment rate is abysmally high."

"Wow, that's really bad."

"Yes. Very bad."

"In Nigeria, and also in Ghana, the direct impact of COVID-19 on individuals cannot be quantified."

"Yes. Even here in Paris, many people who work at restaurants, grocery stores, bars, coffee shops, have been laid off."

"One of my brothers in Ghana called to inform me about his job loss. But what can I do to help him?"

"Very unfortunate. I sympathise with him. Do you have unemployment benefits in Ghana for unemployed people?"

"No. Not at all. No Social Security in Third World countries!"

"What a shame!"

"It breaks my heart that people who had jobs a month ago and could pay their own bills, now have nothing to survive on."

"That's the reality we have found ourselves!"

"I want to boost your immune system."

"How?"

"Through credit alert, of course! There is nothing that awakens someone like credit alert."

"Ummm, you are on point, Dayo. Please boost my immunity against Coronavirus fast."

"Don't worry. I'm sending the money right away..."

Both of us laughed cheerfully and he ended the Zoom meeting. Within five minutes, I got a credit alert on my phone. The amount I saw blew my mind.

CHAPTER
Eleven

There was a knock on my room door. I stood up and went to answer the door, "Yes, who's knocking?"

"It's me, Benson."

"Okay, just a minute."

I opened the door and greeted him, "Benson! Good morning. Good to see you. Please come in."

"Good morning, Pumaya..." He responded.

"How was your night?"

"Fine. And yours?"

"Fine too."

"What are you taking for breakfast? I'm here to take your orders..." Both of us chuckled.

"Wow! You are such a nice guy... Any food is okay by me. But fried yam and plantain with stew will be perfect if you don't mind."

"That's okay by me too."

"What about our friend?"

"Adakole?"

"Yes."

"Oh, he likes and eats any food I prepare. He's not selective or picky about food."

An hour later, breakfast was ready. And we ate with great relish. "Benson, you are a very good cook. You and your future wife will compete for sure... Thank you so much. I always enjoy your meal," I commended.

"Thanks, my pleasure."

"Thank you, Benny," Adakole also complimented. But Benson chuckled and whispered in my ears, "Have you not noticed the name Adakole called me? He called me Benny instead of Benson."

"Ummm, it's true, anytime he feels good about your meal, he tends to call you Benny."

We all started laughing hilariously.

While still on the dining table, Benson said, "I realised that the difficulties of the lockdown has made some of us to engage with technology in a new way. Imagine if there was no virtual platform like Zoom."

I responded, "I concur. Before now, while in Ghana, I was resistant to innovation or cautious about the Internet. But now, I have overcome my fears."

Adakole chipped in, "Suddenly and gradually, Pumaya is becoming a broadcaster. He has hosted a number of Zoom meetings..."

I interjected, "But I'm not internet or Zoom savvy yet. The first Zoom meeting I hosted was a flop or a disaster, as I did not know how to control my participants, share my documents or make the meeting interesting."

"What about me? I have not hosted any Zoom meeting. I only know how to join meetings. But to host a meeting is a different ball game," Benson lamented.

I encouraged him, "My friend, Rome was not built in a day. Just keep trying. Okay?"

"Okay, thanks for your encouragement."

"When the lockdown was announced, some folks thought it was a death sentence or a permanent struggle," Adakole opined.

"The lockdown is not a death sentence! We are surviving it already. And many of us are taking advantage of it," Benson chipped in.

"Yes! It is even working out for our good. It was the lockdown that made us interact with people via Zoom.

The period has even afforded many people the opportunity to rest very well," I opined.

"You can say that again! Even my uncle's friend, Prof. Bala Dogo Fai, whose Blood Pressure was reading high before is now reading normal again, and he is feeling healthy now," Benson contributed.

"Was the professor a workaholic?" I asked.

"Yes, he was. His doctor warned him to slow down but he didn't listen. Now, the lockdown has forced him to slow down a bit..."

"I don't know why some elderly folks are so stubborn. Do you know that many of them don't like taking their prescribed medication?"

"Yes. But why?"

"Maybe because they have seen it all, and they are not afraid of kicking the bucket..."

"Pumaya, Pumaya, your phone is ringing," Adakole notified me.

I quickly rushed into my room to pick up the phone. But before I could do that, the phone had stopped ringing. Alas, it was a missed call from an emerging young footballer, Bidemi Isaac who I met when he came to Ghana on football trials. He was so passionate about playing professional football abroad that nothing else mattered to him. Bidemi was the first to have invited me to Nigeria. But I could not honour his invitation due to personal challenges. Before I could call him back, my phone rang again and I picked it up with excitement.

"Hello, Bidemi. Hello, my dear friend. How are you doing over there in Abuja?"

"I'm fine, and how's Lagos?"

"Lagos is bubbling and sparkling above the flame."

"Ahh, yes Lagos is ever bubbling... Any plans to return to Ghana soon?"

"Not yet. We are still in a lockdown."

"Oh, yes I forgot."

"What about your football career? Has the Coronavirus lockdown affected you in any way?"

"Yes, of course. For me, it has both negative and positive impact. Negative in the sense that I'm unable to express myself on the field. I'm missing the main football action."

"Bidemi, I'm more interested in the positive impact."

"Okay, the positive impact is that I'm improving my skills. I have more time to do personal training, work on my fitness, watch football videos to enhance my skills and mental strength, then I also get to rest..."

"That's splendid. I realised that all over the world, football matches have been put on hold. How do you think players and coaches are faring?"

"Well, football is not just a game, it's a way of life to footballers and coaches. Minimal training is ongoing..."

I interjected, "I agree with you. This morning I went to play football with some boys. It has become a routine for me now."

"Where?"

"Here in Alakuko community. We play on the streets. You know that the lockdown has made Lagos streets free of traffic. I usually join the community boys to exercise."

"That's good Sir. But be careful."

"Ummm, thank you for your concern. You can't believe it, the other day I sustained an injury during training practice."

"Hope you are doing fine Sir?"

"Yes, I'm alive and kicking."

"Good to hear that Sir!"

"But Bidemi, do you think this lockdown is a knockout for you and other players?"

"No. I don't think so. I see this lockdown season as an opportunity to improve myself in the game. All in all, it's a blessing in disguise and we hope to uncover those blessings once all this is over."

"That's great. Nice talking with you."

"Same here Sir."

Late in the night, Benson disrupted my sleep when he came banging on my door and in a moment, I stood up to open for him. "What is the problem? I inquired.

"Pumaya! Pumaya! There is an emergency," he replied with a tremulous voice.

"Ahh! Calm down... What's it?"

"Our neighbour's pregnant wife is in labour... her husband is not around. They need our help..."

"Where has the husband gone to?"

"I don't know."

"Wow, what do we do?"

"We have to rush her to the hospital."

"This night? Don't forget we are in a lockdown. I don't want police trouble."

"There shall be no trouble... Let's go quickly. The woman is in serious pain. You will drive the YDI Mission's vehicle.

"Okay."

Without delay, we picked her and headed toward the hospital where she had been going for antenatal care. I was driving as fast as I could. Benson and the woman's mother were at the back seat of the van, and they were pacifying her.

A few minutes away from the house, some policemen on patrol stopped me. Pronto, I stopped.

"You bastards, where are you going this night?"

"We are not bastards! Emergency Sir. A pregnant woman is in labour, Sir." I replied in annoyance.

One of them used his bright torch-light to search the van. He was drunk and smelling of alcohol. When he opened his mouth to talk, I felt like vomiting because of the foul smell. He asked with a commanding tone, "Woman, are you in labour?"

Mrs Ajayi, the elderly woman replied, "Officer, my daughter is in pains. Please allow us to go."

"Old woman, don't... don't stress us. We are on special duty. How am I even sure this woman is pregnant? This is Lagos, criminals are capable of anything."

Mrs Razaq started screaming and talking, "My husband has left me to suffer alone. Where is the man who is responsible for my condition? Ahhh ah, ah, ah, ah, ah… Ummm, my waist. My back. My tummy. My body... Mummy, am I going to deliver in the vehicle?"

"My daughter, don't worry about that."

Benson and I were panic-stricken. We didn't know what to do. The policemen disappeared into thin air when they discovered that the pregnant woman was about to deliver any moment.

"Madam, now that the policemen have gone should I drive fast to the hospital?" I asked.

"No, the baby is already coming. It's not proper to deliver a baby on motion. Just park off the road."

"I have done that Ma."

"I need water to wash my hands."

"We have some bottles of water in the vehicle. How many bottles do you want Ma?"

"Just one will do."

Benson quickly opened the boot and brought her a bottle of water. She washed her hands and excitedly said, "I'm getting ready to catch my baby."

"Mummy, can you feel my baby's head?"

"Yes..."

"Mummy, I can feel my baby's head engaging."

"Okay, begin to push gently."

"Mummy I feel like defecating."

"That's your baby coming. Just keeping pushing..."

In a moment, the retired nurse calmly caught the baby. And she shouted joyfully, "Congratulations! My daughter, you have a baby boy."

Truly, when Mrs Razaq was about to give birth, her labour pain was extremely excruciating. But when she saw her baby, a new life into the world, her joy knew no bounds. The joy was powerful enough to wipe out the memory of her pain. Apart from the joy of having a baby, she was extremely overwhelmed by the good news of delivering a baby boy. It was an expectation come through and a prayer answered as she had been expecting to have a boy, after having three girls. Most

African wives would love to have boys much more than girls.

The old woman cut the placenta within a few minutes. She did an excellent job of a midwife. After all, she was a retired nursing matron who had delivered many babies in the course of her career that spanned over 35 years. With her long experience in nursing and midwifery, I did not know why she was insisting that her daughter be taken to the hospital after delivery. I asked her, but with great trepidation, "Madam, why don't you just handle everything by yourself?"

"No, my son, it is not proper for me to handle everything. I did not follow the best procedures. The circumstance of the delivery requires post-delivery professional attention."

"Okay Ma."

"Thank you."

"You're welcome Ma."

I drove off, heading to the hospital.

CHAPTER
Twelve

In the morning, our neighbour, Mr Obafemi Razaq came to our apartment to appreciate Benson and me for all the help we rendered to his wife in his absence. He was so elated. And he excitedly thanked us from the depth of his heart. But I questioned him, "Mr Razaq, where did you go? You were not available for your wife..."

He interjected, "My buddy, it's not like that. I went out to pick up some items in readiness for my wife's delivery."

"Okay then."

"But I had issues with my car on my way back home."

"What was it?"

"Ummm, it was a tyre problem."

"Ahh, tyre problem in the night?"

"Yes! And there were no vulcanisers at that odd hour of the night. The lockdown affected them..."

"How did you manage?"

"Umm! Funny enough, even my spare tyre was bad. Double tragedies you would say."

"So, what did you do?" I asked.

"I just drove the car gently until I got home."

"That means the tyre is condemned."

"Absolutely..."

"Wow, it's better that way. You would have been stranded. And even the police might have come there to harass you."

"They actually came, but when they saw my precarious situation, they wished me good luck and drove off..."

"Mr Razaq, it was police wahala that made your wife to deliver in the vehicle. But your mother in-law tried her best to deliver the baby," Benson quipped.

"Benson... Pumaya, you guys tried for me. You are good neighbours. Thank you so much."

"It's our pleasure to help," I responded.

Seven days later, according to Islamic practice, a naming ceremony was organised by Mr Razaq and his wife. But due to the lockdown, friends and family members who could have made the event grandiose did not come. Even the usual slaughter of sheep did not take place. Benson, Adakole and I were on hand to celebrate with the family.

Mrs Razaq who was elegantly dressed and looking gorgeous came from the inner room to the living room where we sat, awaiting her arrival. As soon as she entered, we stood up and greeted her.

She was extremely pleased to see the three of us and she said, "Pumaya... Benson! I'm grateful for your help the other day. Thanks a lot. May Allah reward you."

"It's our pleasure, Madam," I responded with excitement.

Mr Razaq's mother in-law also complimented us:

"I thank both of you for using your Mission's Van to carry us to the hospital. Imagine if there was no vehicle to use that day, could we have trekked to the hospital?"

"We thank God we didn't trek, Mummy," Mrs Razaq responded.

Her mother continued, "I read about a pathetic story of a pregnant woman who went into labour as she struggled towards the hospital on foot. Crumpling in pain from her contractions, her unborn child died en route and she too died the following day."

"Ahh, what a pity! So tragic... That's the negative impact of a lockdown or movement restrictions," I opined.

Mr Razaq made some prayers and blessings on the baby and thereafter announced: "By the power vested in me as the father, I hereby name our baby boy, Musa El-Ruffai Razaq."

Everyone of us repeated the name after him seven times. It was a happy moment for the family. We presented our monetary gifts to the baby and left. But Adakole was still 'lurking around', obviously to see Rahinatu. I began to wonder in my mind what the hell he was doing there. But after 30 minutes, he walked back to our apartment, carrying some food in two big coolers.

Benson, as usual, picked on him, "Adakole, food major. You waited to collect more food from your babe, abi?"

"Ahh, but the food is for two of you. I'm only a courier!"

"But you like food too much..."

"Not only food. He likes Rahinatu too."

"I don't like the way you guys pick on me in this apartment. I'm beginning to sense that two of you don't like me. What have I done to procure your dislike or hatred? If this animosity continues, I will have no option than to report you guys to Mr Jasper Okoko..."

I interjected, "Adakole... It has not come to that. I don't think we dislike or hate you. But the truth is that you and the unemployed sister of Mr Razaq are getting too familiar with each other."

Benson chipped in, "Adakole, please face the fact, you are falling in love with Rahinatu..."

"No! No! Benson, are you saying it's bad to like someone?"

"No. I'm not saying so. Don't you think it's because of proximity or the lockdown?"

"I don't understand."

"The lockdown helps two of you to see each other every day. It is generating closeness or proximity. She has visited our apartment to ask for you many times."

"My dear Adakole, be careful! Can you handle the inter-religious relationship?"

Adakole with a depressed look, responded, "You guys are jumping the gun. When we get to the bridge we will know how to cross it..."

"Don't be moved by her beauty. Character is superior to beauty..."

"Yes, yes my friend. I don't think Rahinatu has a good character."

"How do you know?" Adakole promptly queried.

"She has been fighting and quarrelling with her sister in-law, Mrs Taiwo Rasaq every now and then."

"Please don't judge her. She does most of the work in that house. Is it because she is jobless? The Madam is mean to her..."

In the evening, in order to contend with the lockdown boredom, I urged my friends to join me and the community boys to play football on our street corner. But Adakole opined, "You are talking of playing football with the boys when most of them are starving. The immediate impact of the lockdown on the boys is lack of food. Why don't you donate your food to them?"

"Yes. I don't mind," I responded.

In a moment, an idea of giving food palliative flooded my mind. But my greatest challenge was how to source for food. That same night while bubbling with the idea of adding value to Alakuko community, I quickly called and shared the vision with Moses Ayua, Koffi and his wife, and a few others. I asked them to buy into my vision. I told them about the urgency of the project. Debo, a friend of mine in the UK was the first to send some money. Others followed suit.

No doubt, the lockdown was becoming like hell to so many impoverished people in Alakuko. I was thankful to Adakole, whose idea birthed my Charity Initiative in Lagos. I did not see what he saw at first, but I later saw a need to help out. When I began the initiative, my friends and I had nothing much, but we were determined to make big sacrifices to tackle hunger among our community residents.

CHAPTER
Thirteen

Within five days, under the auspices of my Charity Initiative, we were able to purchase 350 small bags of rice, 50 big bags of beans, 1000 tubers of yam, 450 cartons of biscuits and noodles, 65 cartons of milk and 2000 loaves of bread for distribution to Alakuko community residents. Many of my donors gave in kind; some supplied hand sanitisers, face masks and toiletries in addition to food items which they donated.

I mobilised volunteers from the community to assist my team and me in maintaining peace and to guard against any form of stampede. I put them under the supervision of Mr Razaq who had been a community leader of some sort. He was a one-time chairman of Alakuko Community Development Association. Being an indigene and resident of the locality who understood the culture and language of the people, it was wise of me to have engaged him.

During the distribution of the palliatives, I watched Alakuko community residents smiling and jubilating. I was even moved to tears when an elderly woman told me that she and her children had not eaten for days. So, when she got her ration she was highly appreciative. Many others walked up to me, thanking and appreciating me. I was taken aback for their display of gratitude. Their thankful attitude or disposition was greatly instructive.

I asked Benson why the people were so appreciative. He responded, "Pumaya, it is a cultural thing. A typical Yoruba person will thank or appreciate you for every act of good you've done for him or her..."

"Wow! That's a good culture!"

"The people believe that if they thank you for a good deed done to them, they are actually applying for more good deeds in future."

"Ummm, I like that."

"You've learnt a true life principle from Lagos."

"Yes. I'm going to be more appreciative to God and man beginning from now!"

A day later, I called Debo and shared with him my joy of living a life of contribution, not a life of consumption.

"Hi, Debo, you can't imagine or describe the joy of my heart."

"How do you mean?"

"I mean, I'm so joyous for putting smiles on faces!"

"Okay, yes it is great to do that."

"Debo, I'm most thankful for your financial support. God will reward you."

"Amen! My pleasure, Pumaya."

"I will send you some pictures soon."

"That's great. That will be nice..."

"I'm proud of the project I championed in Lagos. I plan to replicate the same project in Ghana after the lockdown."

"Be rest assured of my support. You've done a great job in Nigeria. Your adventure or mission in Lagos is never in vain."

Smiling, I said, "Yes, I'm a proud adventurist! As a first-timer in Lagos, I was not afraid to step out to make a difference. When I left Tamale for Lagos, I did not have the faintest idea that I was going to add value to poor folks in Alakuko community. Even in the midst of the lockdown, I was able to touch lives."

"Truly, it takes an adventurist to venture into the unknown terrain to make a difference. I promise to help you make contacts with charities here in UK with similar vision. You need to take this initiative to another level... I will call you tomorrow."

"Okay. That will be nice of you Debo. I'll appreciate that."

"Bravo... Bye Pumaya."

"Bye, Debo."

As soon as I was done speaking with Debo, I picked Koffi's call. He greeted me and asked, "Pumaya, what's up? How did your event go?"

"Very fine. It went perfectly well."

"Hope you were very fulfilled... "

"Yes, I was fulfilled and I'm still fulfilled. There is nothing so thrilling and fulfilling like making another human being happy."

"Pumaya, I'm happy for you."

"Thank you for your support... Let me forward some pictures of the event to you via WhatsApp."

"Okay, please send the pictures."

"I will do just that. What about your wife and kids? I love your kids. They are very sharp like you, Koffi."

"Thanks! Do you know that Jumoke and I had planned to smuggle you?"

"Me?"

"Yes."

"To Ghana?"

"No! To our house... We wanted you to spend some time with us!"

"Ahh..."

"But our plans did not work out as we planned it."

"Wow, that would have been nice, but you guys wouldn't have smuggled me as I was very busy over here. Do you know that my initiative is gaining and receiving acceptance with the Lagos State government? I got some support from them."

"Wow, you don't mean it."

"I mean it. Our neighbour, Mr Rasaq was highly supportive. He was the person who linked me to the State government and I have been eminently helped."

"That's a good one, Pumaya. To find someone like that is rare."

"Yes, Mr Razaq is an advocate of religious harmony and tolerance. He was the one who told me that two former Lagos State Governors had Christian wives. That's an epitome of religious harmony."

"My brother, leave that matter. It could be a political strategy."

"Koffi, but they were married before they became governors."

"My brother, I have been living in Lagos for years... Leave that matter. You don't know politicians. They are capable of anything..."

"I don't think so... I don't think it is a political strategy. I think it is a cultural thing. On our street here in Alakuko, there is a church built adjacent to a mosque. And there is no schism..."

"Yes, I give that to Yoruba people. In many Yoruba families and neighbourhoods, you will find Christians and Muslims living together with great tolerance. No doubt, their level of religious harmony is high and should be emulated."

"One of the values I discovered here is religious harmony and I'm taking it to Northern Ghana, to Tamale specifically."

"Yes, you guys need religious harmony and tolerance there. I learnt how you were nearly killed by religious bigots."

"My brother, it was a huge persecution. Even up till now, I still face issues with some fundamentalists."

"Pumaya, are you still going back to Ghana? What will happen to your Charity Initiative? Your hands are already full with activities and projects over here in Lagos."

"Yes, but I will still go back to Ghana! My friends and Mr Razaq will continue with the Initiative. My assignment is not here in Nigeria. The moment the lockdown is relaxed, I will jet out for Accra. I'm missing my wife badly."

Koffi chuckled and teased me: "Pumaya, you are missing your wife, because you have been sex-starved..."

"No! No! Koffi, don't be naughty..."

"I'm not naughty. I know what you are losing. Since you came to Lagos you have lost sexual intimacy with your wife."

"No doubt, sexual intimacy contributes to the physical, emotional, social and even mental health of couples. But for now, I've decided to take off my mind..."

"Take off your mind from sex?"

"Yes!"

"But I can't!"

"You can."

"How?"

"Get busy with some valuable projects 24/7. Saturate your mind with great thoughts and imaginations. Become spiritual. Get involved in reading..."

"Enough, enough, my lecturer brother. I will talk to you tomorrow."

"Okay. My regards to Jumoke and kids."

"Bye Pumaya!"

"Bye Koffi."

Two weeks later, Lagos State government announced partial relaxation of the lockdown. And that meant Lagos residents could move about freely but with strict standards and rules. The announcement of the relaxation brought us much happiness. So much so that Benson announced to Adakole and me, "Announcement! Announcement! My great buddies, now that we are free to move around, it would not be a bad idea if we go get some money from the bank. I need some money to buy some foodstuff."

"That's a good idea," I concurred.

"Benson! Can I go with you?" Adakole requested.

"No, you stay back with our Ghanaian friend. Let me rush there and come back quickly."

"Okay, if you say so," Adakole agreed.

"Point of information, Mrs Jasper Okoko promised to give some food supplies..."

"To us or to your charity work?" Benson asked.

"To us of course... I suggest Adakole should go to her house and pick up the supplies, while I stay back to tidy up our apartment."

"That's cool, you are a neat guy. I like your neat room."

"Thanks. I can't stand a dirty environment..."

"That means you can't stand Lagos! This city is dirty," Adakole interjected.

"But residents are responsible! It is a people thing. Not a government thing. Residents dump refuse anyhow and anywhere."

"No. I don't subscribe to that. Government is responsible... Pumaya, you're becoming a government enthusiast..."

"No! No! I'm not! I'm just talking from personal observations."

"Pumaya, is Accra that dirty too?

"No. Compared to Lagos, Accra is as neat as a new pin, and more organised. My friend, in Accra, indiscriminate dumping of refuse is not allowed. There is a heavy penalty if you do."

"Wow, I like that. Here, everyone is allowed to do whatever they like. Have you been to slums in Lagos?"

"No."

"I suggest that you visit some places before you go back to Accra. Places like Oshodi, Ajegunle, Okokomaiko..."

"Ahh! Is Mr Jasper Okoko from Okokomaiko?

"No. I don't think so."

"Benson, will you take me to those places? I'd like to visit Banana Island, we've heard so much about that Estate back in Ghana. It's my dream estate to visit."

Adakole responded with an air of pride, "Banana Island is Nigeria's most expensive and extravagant estate to visit if you want to broaden your horizons. But the security to enter there is tight; no poor person is allowed. Mr Adekinki took some students there and they were turned back. They decided to drive around Park View Estate in Ikoyi and returned to Igando feeling so distraught... Pumaya, are there such exclusive estates in Accra?"

"No! But you know Nigeria is richer than Ghana and you have more wealthy people in Nigeria. Don't forget that the richest African is a Nigerian."

Adakole excused himself. He went to the restroom to ease himself, and within a few minutes, he was back to continue his discussion, "Pumaya, I will visit Accra one day."

"That will be nice! You will love the city. Accra has a small population compared to Lagos."

"I don't like the overpopulation of Lagos. It's like all Nigerians are trooping into Lagos. The amenities in Lagos are being overstretched."

"Adakole, business is the source of attraction. People come into Lagos in huge numbers to do business! One good thing is that if you are not lazy you can survive in Lagos."

"It's true. Let me go and have my bath."

"Please do."

In a moment, Benson came out of his room, sanitised his hands and put on a funny-looking face mask in readiness to go to the bank. The Lagos State government had made the use of face masks compulsory for anyone going out to public places. The three of us had bought different types of face masks for use throughout the COVID-19 crisis.

Benson stood at the bus stop for nearly 30 minutes waiting for unavailable buses. Commuters rushed to board a few half-empty buses popularly called 'danfos' in Lagos. One astounding thing was that many people were not adhering to the social distancing rule; they were fighting themselves and rushing to board the limited 'danfos' to their destinations. Benson decided to join the bandwagon to secure a seat. But he was unsuccessful and he blamed himself for not praying enough before stepping out.

He convinced himself that it was not too late to pray: "Oh Lord, I'm sorry I didn't pray fervently before I rushed out this morning. Please forgive me. Lord, favour me. Protect me against this Coronavirus. Oh God, arise and preserve me in Jesus mighty Name." He whispered a heartfelt prayer to God. Not too long after his prayer, a private taxi, popularly called 'kabukabu' in Lagos stopped for him; he boarded and began negotiating with the driver, "Please how much to Egbeda?"

The driver responded, "My brother, I'm just helping you. Don't bother paying..."

"Ahh, that's kind of you, God bless you real good. I really appreciate you."

"Don't bother thanking me, just thank God!"

On getting to the bank, Benson was flabbergasted to see a mammoth crowd of bank customers all over the bank premises. He wondered in his mind, whether he would succeed in completing his banking transactions on such a busy day. "What am I seeing here? No social distancing here! Can I stand this?" He wondered aloud.

A bank customer tapped him on the shoulder; and he reacted angrily, "What's the matter? Why are you touching me? Don't you know about social distancing?"

"Sorry Sir. I wanted to ask a question Sir."

"Can't you ask your question without touching somebody? What's your question?"

"Please Sir, your dressing is like that of a banker. Could you please help me? I have been here since 6 a.m. but people are simply unruly. No one is respecting the social distancing rule at all. See the way they are falling upon one another..."

"Sorry, I can't help you. I'm not a banker. I'm here like you."

"Sir, what is the essence of putting on face masks when people are pushing one another in order to get into the banking hall?"

"I don't know. I think we need more law enforcement officers to compel customers to adhere strictly to the rules."

"For sure, we need leaders who will strictly uphold rules with iron hands in this country."

Benson could not achieve any result due to the chaotic situation at the bank. He came back home, feeling so distressed and frustrated. But I became a shoulder for him to lean on. I encouraged him, and he resolved to go back to the bank early enough the following day.

When he learned from a bank customer of how she got to the bank as early as 6 a.m. the previous day, Benson decided to be in the bank, latest by 5:30 a.m. on this day. He was over the moon because he was able to reach the bank on time. The chaotic situations had subsided drastically, as bank customers were given numbers as they came into the bank premises. His number was eight! So he was among the first ten people who were called in. Without much hassles, he completed his transaction and left for home.

Upon his arrival, Benson went straight to the kitchen to fix food for us. His spirit or grace of service was superior to mine. And I deliberately and purposefully decided to connect with the spirit of servant-hood he carried. No doubt, the next level of my life will require a different version of me. The old version of me, that was self-centred must be jettisoned for the 'new me' who possess selfless service to emerge.

CHAPTER

Fourteen

A few days after, the Ghanaian embassy in Lagos apprised me of our government's plan to evacuate citizens stranded in Nigeria. I quickly informed my buddies of the plan. "Guys, my government is planning evacuation and I like to take advantage of it," I enthused. Benson immediately made a good suggestion. He said, "That's a nice plan. But you can't go without a send-off party."

"That's thoughtful of you..." I commended him.

"It will be a good idea to do the party at the beach," Benson further suggested.

"Beach?" Adakole asked.

"Yes, Alpha beach will be okay."

I consented, "It will be a memorable outing to experience. How do we go about it?"

"Leave that to me. I will fix it," Benson boasted.

Benson had a knack for event planning and execution. He invited MC Touchnot, the comedian who had visited us before to add flavour to our outing. Without consultation with me or Benson, Adakole went ahead to invite Rahinatu Razaq for the beach party. I was not comfortable about her following us. I personally confronted Adakole, "Why did you invite Rahinatu to my party without interfacing with me?"

"I'm sorry but you know she assisted Benson in the kitchen..."

"It doesn't mean."

"Okay. I'm sorry."

"Let me talk to her!"

As soon as Rahinatu came into our apartment I confronted her, "Rahinatu, I'm not comfortable with your coming to the beach with us."

"Ahh, but why?" She asked, looking disturbed. "Because you will be the only lady in our midst."

"Ahh, Pumaya, it doesn't matter."

"It does."

"Okay. Please let my friend come with me. She's been with me in our house for quite some time now."

"Yes, I have seen her a couple of times. But we don't know her personally."

"But I know her. She is a good girl. Trust me."

"Okay."

"Let's be on our way. Pumaya, you will be on the steering," Benson urged me.

"But I don't have a driver's licence..." I protested.

"But you drove to the hospital the other day."

"It was an emergency situation, you know."

"Okay. Don't worry, I will be on the steering."

It was a jolly ride from Alakuko, as we were chatting and cracking jokes with reckless abandon. But Benson's driving was nauseating to me, as he was doing the 'slow and steady' type of driving. He was not smart and calculative, rather he was very sluggish in manoeuvring, navigating Lagos traffic and dodging pot-holes. We even had near-accident incidents on our way. As if that was not enough, we had social infraction with some Lagos hawkers who aggressively marketed their wares. They were virtually compelling us to buy their stuff.

Benson informed me, "Pumaya, we are passing through the popular Third Mainland Bridge."

"Wow, I learnt it's the longest bridge in Africa."

"No, it's no longer the longest in Africa. It was the longest bridge in Africa until 1996 when the 6th October Bridge located in Cairo was completed..."

"You can't link Lagos Island and Lekki-Ajah axis without passing through the Third Mainland Bridge which has now become a notorious spot for suicides. Many lives have been wasted on the bridge," Rikiya interjected.

"Rikiya, it's true. I remember passing through the bridge on my way to my cousin's house the other day. And the Uber driver mentioned the same thing about suicide cases on the bridge."

"Pumaya! Apart from the menace of suicide, the security challenge on the bridge is another thing. Many motorists have been robbed. Others have been killed by robbers," Adakole contributed.

"Security challenge is a city-wide thing," I sharply responded.

"Yes ooo! This is Lagos for you! Security is a tough matter in Lagos!" Rahinatu interjected.

I replied snappingly, "Not only Lagos. It's a national quagmire."

"Have you passed through the Lekki-Ikoyi link bridge?" Benson asked.

"No."

"It is a beautiful 1.36 km cable-stayed bridge which links the Phase 1 area of Lekki, with Ikoyi district."

"Can we pass through it?"

"Why not."

"The bridge is one of the finest Lagos landmarks; to the point that our Nollywood film makers have overused or stereotyped it in their films."

"That's the problem with us Nigerians, we like over flogging things," Rahinatu opined.

"Apart from vehicular traffic, the bridge also serves as a recreational facility," Benson continued.

"Like how?" I asked with stupefaction.

"Fitness inclined residents of Lekki phase 1 and Ikoyi use the wide curbs of the bridge for jogging and running, usually in the early mornings and evenings."

"That's splendid. I like that."

"As an adventurist, you have to visit the bridge like other tourists and visitors have done in the past."

"Can't we pass through it?"

"Yes, we can."

"I'd like to take some snapshots there. Would I be permitted to take pictures?"

"Yes. It's a public bridge. I think it is now becoming the most photographed place in Lagos..."

Rahinatu excitedly chipped in, "Even Mark Zuckerberg, the Facebook mogul went on a morning run on the Bridge during his visit to Lagos."

"Wow! Rahinatu, that was cool."

"Mark's pictures and video clips on the bridge went viral on social media, especially on Facebook and Instagram."

"Umm, that's the social media boss himself."

We parked our vehicle at the Lekki end of the beautiful bridge. All of us trekked on the bridge curbs to take pictures. Rahinatu and Rikiya joined me to take selfies. I took loads of personal selfies.

I called and engaged a passerby to help me take group pictures and he gladly obliged me. And it was fun capturing beautiful buildings and bridges on our way.

Without further ado, I started uploading my beautiful pictures on social media.

As we were approaching the gate of Alpha Beach, along Ajah-Lekki axis, a band of youths, popularly called Area boys in Lagos, armed with sticks and all manner of traditional 'missiles' stopped us and demanded: "Give us 5k, if not, you will not go in."

"Is that the gate fee?" Rahinatu and MC Touchnot asked simultaneously.

"No be gate fee, na our own. Na area money be that," they explained in pidgin English.

"We are not prepared for any extra expenses," Benson responded with great venom.

Pronto, a fierce argument ensued, and before anyone could say, 'Jack Robinson,' one of the bad boys smashed our windscreen with an object.

Benson alighted from the vehicle to inspect the damage. I joined him to challenge the rough guy, "Young man, why did you smash our windscreen?"

The guy responded, "Who are you?"

"It's not a matter of who am I, it's a matter of the damage you caused to our vehicle..."

Before I knew it, the bad boy gave me a dirty slap. I responded with the same intensity. He punched my nose. His evil companions teamed up against me. I could not match their combined strength. Before my co-fun seekers could come to my rescue, they lifted me up and hit me on the beach sand. They started raining blows on me. I screamed in pains.

Rahinatu took a bottle and broke it on her head. When they saw the weird display of self-harm, they got scared. With the broken bottle in her hand, she ran after them like a wounded lioness. She pinned one of them down, using her weight to suffocate the boy.

She was shouting: "I'll kill you. You bastard, you homeless idiot. You don't know me, I'm a buccaneer. Touch me, you're dead!"

Adakole, Benson and MC Touchnot joined in the free-for-all fight. The fracas became bloody as the Area boys were using broken bottles, sticks and other missiles freely to cause us bodily harm. We did the same to them!

Before the beach security could come to disentangle the barbarous boys from us and quell the fight, so much damage had been done. But on sighting the police, they disappeared into thin air. We were no more in the mood for any beach party as we had to go to a nearby clinic for medical care. I had a minor cut on my head, which was treated and bandaged. Others sustained minor injuries and they were given pain relievers. I was proud of the gallantry of Rahinatu. She was like the biblical Deborah who stood up to defend Israel against King Jabin's army.

When we got home, we decided to eat and entertain ourselves with jokes in our apartment. Not minding my bandaged head, I was ebullient, making everyone happy. MC Touchnot said, "Pumaya! This bandage will remind you that you truly adventured into Lagos! This is Lagos; where Area boys and girls are lords in their area! They are feared by many normal people..."

"But why?"

"I don't know!"

"Lagos is full of absurdities!"

"Grammar! What do you mean?"

"I mean to say that Lagos is ridiculous. So many illogical or nonsensical things happen here."

"This is Lagos! The good and the ugly, the first-rate and last-rate cohabit here. That's the irrationality of the highest order!"

Rahinatu and her friend helped to serve us fried rice. As she was serving, her brother, Mr Razaq came in to celebrate with me. His sister served him respectfully. But as he was biting his chicken, a splash of stew entered his eyes. He screamed, "My eyes, my eyes..." Quickly, I ran into the bathroom and brought him water and soap to wash his eyes. We felt sorry for him. He did not finish his food, but left feeling bad.

MC Touchnot praised Rahinatu for her service and bravery that she displayed at the beach. He said, "My guys, Rahinatu should be given an award for her bravery and for being streetwise! She is a defender of the universe..."

Rahinatu objected, "I'm not a defender of the universe, God is! Don't ever ascribe God's quality to any man."

"I'm only joking."

"But don't joke like that. Allah is the greatest!"

Rahinatu excused herself and left with her friend, Rikiya.

"Men, that lady is a fighter!" Benson opined.

I responded, "Yes. She is. I pity Adakole. She will use her big body and fighting skill to discipline Adakole. Did you guys hear when she said she was a buccaneer?"

"Yes. I heard and I was taken aback. Rahinatu is a cultist... Ahh, I will use diplomacy to tactically disconnect from her," Adakole declared.

Meanwhile, in the night of the incident, Rahinatu and her friend, Rikiya were discussing me and the incident at the beach.

"Rahibaby, you really tried," Rikiya teased her friend.

"Tried like how?"

"You tried to impress the guys with your stunts."

"Not the guys but Adakole in particular. I love the guy. I want to date him and I am effusive about it. I don't know how to express my desire to him. We are fond of each other but he has not asked me out formally. What do I do to woo or seduce him? Any idea from you?"

"Love portion of course!"

"How do I go about it?"

"Don't worry. We will consult that Baba in Ijebu Ode. But as for me, I'm attracted to Pumaya. That guy is fine. I wouldn't mind being his Nigerian babe. I can do anything to have him..."

Rahinatu interrupted her, "No space for you there."

"Why?"

"He's married. Like I told you the other day, he is in love with his wife. He talks about her all the time."

"I don't care! Whether he is married or not, I want him. Give me one or two weeks, and I will trap him."

"Rikiya, I warn you, leave the Ghanaian guy alone... Why not go for Benson or the comedian?"

"No, they are not my type. I can't wait for Pumaya to squeeze me to submission."

"Hey, Rikiya! You are lusting after him."

"No! I'm loving him..."

"This is not love. This is infatuation! This is madness!"

"But I can't help myself."

"You better help yourself... Let's sleep."

"I can't! I can't manage my thoughts. This guy is on my mind 24/7! I have never felt like this for any guy lately."

"My dear Rikiya! That guy is hyper-spiritual. He won't cheat on his wife. I'm sure of this."

"How do you know? Have you tried him before?"

"No! I beg you, leave me out of your bizarre or crazy lust. Good night, my friend."

"Good night. Sleep well, if mosquitoes will allow you. Mosquitoes in Alakuko are giant dragons!"

"My friend, you can say that again..."

Meanwhile, Rikiya was still restless and sleepless. She went into a hysterical and weird soliloquy:

"Pumaya! Pumaya! I want you! I'm ready for your love. Come to me, I want to see your face, let me hear your voice. For your voice is soothing and your face is ravishing. Oh, Pumaya! I'm tormented here. You are sleeping calmly now but I'm restless in bed and sleepless. Pumaya, I long for you. I want you desperately. Only you can quench this thirst of my heart. Get up, Pumaya! My handsome dude. Kiss me just once and that will suffice, that will be sufficient, that will be okay! Pumaya! Pumaya! I'm madly in love with you..."

A week after the beach incident, I was set to depart Nigeria for Ghana. Virtually every night, we would talk and crack jokes till the early hours of the morning. We also had time to pray and commit our various ministries and projects into God's hands. We discussed the good times and the various experiences we shared during the height of the lockdown. We were happy for one another as we stayed together with minimal conflicts throughout the lockdown.

Now it was time for us to say goodbye to one another.

Benson said, "Pumaya, I will miss you."

"I will miss you too, Benson..."

I turned to Adakole and held his two hands and said, "My brother, you made my adventure in Lagos an interesting one. Without you, I wouldn't have added value to Alakuko community. And I wouldn't have had a life project to run with. Apart from my mission work, I now have a Charity Initiative to cater for the less-privileged people in Makayili and Tamale."

Adakole responded, "Pumaya, your heart is golden! With all the sufferings and challenges, you remained positive. I will surely miss you."

He broke down and burst into tears. I sharply rebuked him, "No! Don't break my heart, Adakole. You're being emotional... Comport yourself. Okay?"

I embraced him. His tears flowed freely, and my striped T-shirt got wet with his tears.

In the morning, before we left for the airport, I received a phone call from Mrs Okoko. She said, "Finally the storm is over!"

"Yes Ma!"

"Don't forget to pay extra attention to the health and hygiene rules at the airport."

"Yes Ma!"

"Do you have a hand sanitiser?"

"Yes Ma, the one you sent to me is still available Ma."

"I advise that you take along your own germicidal wipes to rub-down the high-touch surfaces, like the armrest."

"But I don't have such wipes Ma."

"Okay. Don't worry. The airline might supply that. But if not, your hand sanitiser will suffice."

"Okay Ma. Thank you for your love and generous gifts that kept us going during the lockdown. And thank you also for supporting my Charity Initiative project. Thank you for everything Ma."

"My pleasure. Please extend our greetings to your wife, and Moses Ayua, your Nigerian friend in Accra."

"I will do just that Ma. My best wishes to Daddy. Bye Ma."

"Bye Pumaya!"

CHAPTER

Fifteen

We left Alakuko, an outskirt community in Lagos early enough to catch my flight at the Murtala Mohammed International Airport. But we did not envisage a terrible traffic that early morning. The traffic was moving at a snail speed. All of a sudden, the traffic stopped moving completely. It was a standstill! The situation became unbearable and I started panicking.

"Benson, what do I do now?" I asked apprehensively.

"Let's pray that the traffic moves..."

"Yes, let's pray. I can't afford to miss this flight."

"Don't worry, you won't miss it."

"Okay, I believe... my guys, I love Lagos but I can't stand the chaotic traffic situation. Okada operators are a menace."

"Yes, but in situations like this, they are useful. Can you try them?"

"Like how?"

"Fly Okada of course!"

"Ahh! Don't forget our last experience with this Okada..."

"Guys, let's hope for the best. We still have time. Lagos traffic can build up so heavy but before you know it, it will disappear. This one will soon disappear," Adakole chipped in.

A few minutes later, the traffic started moving as predicted by Adakole but not fast enough. I opted for Okada bike instead. But none of the operators was willing to carry me. And this was because they were debarred from plying around the airport vicinity for security reasons.

I noticed that the root cause of Lagos traffic mayhem could be attributed to poor driving skills and the unruly behaviour of Lagos drivers; coupled with huge commuters who rush or junket to enter limited buses, not to mention the case of numerous pot-holes. Lagos! Lagos, a city in need of renewal!

When I saw some travellers trekking with their luggage on their heads, I decided to join them to trek too. Benson advised Adakole to accompany and assist me; a piece of advice which Adakole embraced fully. As we were trekking, I was busy praying inwardly for favour. After Iyana-Ipaja axis, I was able to get help from unexpected quarter, as a God-sent military man volunteered to pick me on his bike straight to the airport. I wanted to appreciate him with money but he declined. He wished me a safe trip and left.

The boarding procedure was smooth and stress-free; maybe because it was a special evacuation flight. The Customs and Immigration Services were on hand to make our boarding stress-free. As a first-time traveller, I took a cue from other travellers; how they were comporting themselves. I saw some travellers strolling up and down, but I was not prepared for that, rather I sat not too far from my gate pass area.

About half an hour prior to take-off, the gate attendant announced the boarding time. I was confused as the boarding was done in groups and I did not know the group I belonged to. I had to ask a co-traveller, "Bros I don't know what's going on here."

"Oh, please check your boarding pass to see if you belong to the group being called..."

The tall and dark guy whose beards looked like that of a Taliban glimpsed into my boarding pass and said, "Thank your stars, we are in the same group. Just follow me. Okay?"

"Okay. Thank you Sir."

"Pleasure is mine. Is this your first time?"

"Yes Sir."

"That's great. You will enjoy your flight for sure."

The baldheaded gate attendant checked my boarding pass and queried me, "Where is your International passport, Mr David Pumaya Abdulai?"

"Oh, sorry Sir, I don't have it here, but I have my ECOWAS ID."

"We don't normally accept this means of identification, but, because of the emergency situation of the evacuation, we are compelled to accept. But let me see it."

The attendant sighted my ID and asked me to proceed for boarding. But typically, a build-up of passengers after the boarding pass check made me and my newfound friend wait in line again before boarding the plane.

I located my seat, placed my hand luggage in the overhead bin closest to me. I sat back to relax without fixing my seat belt. And this was because I had issues putting it together. But a pretty female flight-attendant noticed me struggling with the belt and decided to assist me by directing me to watch the in-flight videos showing passengers how to put on their seat belts.

I was listening with rapt attention to the announcement being made.

The announcer who spoke with a female voice said, "Ladies and gentlemen, the Captain has turned on the 'Fasten Seat Belt' sign. If you haven't already done so, please stow your carry-on luggage underneath the seat in front of you or in an overhead bin. Please take your seat and fasten your seat belt. Please make sure your folding trays are properly tucked in and your seat is in full upright position for take-off. If you are seated next to an emergency exit, please read carefully the special instructions card located in your seat pocket. If you do not wish to perform the functions described in the event of an emergency, please ask a flight attendant to reseat you. We remind you that this is a non-smoking flight. Smoking is prohibited on the entire aircraft, including the lavatories. Tampering with, disabling or destroying the lavatory smoke detectors is prohibited by law. If you have any questions about our flight today, please don't hesitate to ask one of our flight attendants. Thank you."

Before we could rest from the first announcement, a second one came on: "Ladies and gentlemen, the Captain has turned off the 'Fasten Seat Belt' sign, and you may now move around the cabin. However, we always recommend keeping your seat belt fastened while you're seated."

In a few moments, the flight attendants came to serve hot or cold drinks as preferred by the passengers, as well as snacks, but I declined the offer.

Even though I had eased myself at the airport, I still wanted to capture the interior of aircraft restrooms. I stood up, excused myself and proceeded to the one at the rear of the plane.

The last major announcement was when we landed safely: "Ladies and gentlemen, welcome to Kotoka International Airport. Local time is 9:55 am and the temperature is 30 degrees Celsius. For your safety and comfort, please remain seated with your seat belt fastened until the Captain turns off the 'Fasten Seat Belt' sign. This will indicate that we have parked at the gate and that it is safe for you to move about. At this time, you may use your cellular phones if you wish. Please check around your seat for any personal belongings you may have brought on board with you and please exercise caution when opening the overhead bins, as heavy articles may have shifted around during the flight. On behalf of Ghana Airlines and the entire crew, I'd like to thank you for joining us on this special trip and we look

forward to having you on board in the nearest future.
Have a nice stay in Accra!"

At the arrival lounge, we started protesting the
quarantine plan of the Ghana Health Agency tasked with
the mandate to curb the spread of the Coronavirus. A
huge man with the mephitic mouth was shouting at us
uncontrollably. Without any sense of decorum, he said,
"File out immediately into the bus packed outside
there..." He pointed to where the bus was. And he
continued, "We don't have much time to waste..."

Some passengers were not pleased with his approach.
They mildly revolted. They refused to go out. The man
came up again with more ferocious vitriol, "You must
behave yourselves. Gently enter into the bus or you will
be forced into it..."

A female frustrated passenger yelled at him, "You can't
do such a thing. We are adults. You can't force us
against our will."

Another officer of the Agency stepped forward to calm
down the nerves of already agitated passengers. He said,
"Fellow compatriots, we know how so many of you
suffered in Nigeria due to the lockdown. The truth is
that, you all have passed through hell, so to say, but the
condition for your evacuation is that you will be
quarantined upon arrival. You are coming from a
country which is exposed to Coronavirus and some of

you may have contracted the contagious disease without knowing or may have the disease but do not show symptoms. After fourteen days, you will be set free to rejoin your family. I want you to understand that our government's action is for the good of your family and Ghanaian people. Please, I urge you to cooperate with us..."

At this juncture, I rose up to the occasion by appealing to my fellow passengers to cooperate with the agency. Finally, we all agreed but some were still murmuring. An officer of the Agency led us into the bus.

CHAPTER

Sixteen

On getting to the Quarantine Centre, we all alighted from the bus and were filed out like prisoners into our allocated rooms. Meanwhile, some onlookers were shaking their heads in disgust or astonishment. They were wondering why we should be treated in such a manner. The only thing that separated us from criminal suspects was that we were not handcuffed.

My heart panted with alarms, and I was wondering what would become of us. I asked myself inwardly, "Would we spend up to fourteen days in this Centre? Why would security personnel be watching and guarding us?" As I was pondering in my heart, a call came in from Benson, my Nigerian friend.

"Hello, Pumaya!"

"Hi Benson. How are you guys doing in Lagos?"

"We are doing fine. And you?"

"We are not fine. You can't believe it... All passengers from Lagos are being quarantined here."

"Ahh! That's not fair. Are you guys sick?"

"No! It is for the good of our families; so they told us."

"But are you guys being taken care of by the government?"

"Yes. They are trying. But I learnt that we might be forced to reimburse the government later."

"Why?"

"I don't know, my friend."

"Hello, hello, I can't hear you well..."

"It's a network problem. Can you hear me now?"

"Yes. But your voice is not clear enough. A bit louder please."

"Okay..."

"Yea, I can hear you now, loud and clear... What about your wife?"

"I was about calling her before your call came in."

"Ahh! Please let me end the call, so you can call her. Extend my best wishes to her."

"Okay. Thank you for checking on me. That's kind of you. My regards to Adakole."

"My pleasure. I will do just that."

I laid down on a four-by-six bed in my room. I joyfully placed a call to my wife, "Hello. Hello. My damsel, I'm back to Ghana..."

My wife excitedly responded, "Wow! That's great! Thank God, you arrived safely."

"Yes, we thank God. And how are you faring?"

"I'm doing fine! When are you coming to Tamale?"

"I don't know yet."

"Why? Do you have any ministration in Accra?"

"No! We are quarantined here in Accra by the government. They gave us a hint about this in Lagos but we did not take them seriously."

"But why?" She started crying. I tried to calm her down but she would not stop crying. She said in tears, "If I had known this journey would cause us so many headaches and heartaches, I would not have supported it."

"But I'm back now. After the expiration of the fourteen days time lag, we will be together again. You have tried, no doubt."

"Fourteen what? You mean I will not see you soon. Oh my love, my husband! I miss you so much. Even your boy in my womb is missing your touch of love," she sobbed uncontrollably. At this point, I broke down in tears, as I could not bear the soul-stirring display of my wife. Both of us cried freely.

The Centre was a beehive of activities as some 'inmates' were being released and other prospective 'inmates' were bundled into the Centre intermittently. I stood at the balcony watching the drama and catching the fun. I saw an elderly woman of about 65 years who sat down with her eyes looking upwards as if she was an eagle looking into the sky. She was hysterical. At a point, she shouted. At another point, she talked to herself in a funny way. I summoned the courage to approach her. I greeted her, "Good evening Madam. How are you?"

She replied, "Good evening my son! Please are you part of the people that dragged me into this Centre meant for criminals?"

"No Ma."

"Who are you?"

"I'm a fellow passenger like you."

"See my legs, I'm chained like a common criminal."

"No Ma. There's no chain on you."

"Look at handcuffs on my hands."

"No Ma. There are no handcuffs..."

The elderly woman sharply interrupted me, "Get out of my presence! Do you have eyes?"

I stepped away from her. She began to scream as if she was in pains. She cried out, "My handcuffs are hurting me real bad. These policemen are wicked. With all the injuries they inflicted on me, they are not satisfied. They want to keep torturing me...," she started sobbing.

I took up her case, having realised that she was suffering from acute depression or insanity. After praying for her, I went a step further by lodging a formal complaint to the authorities of the Centre.

I went to see the officer in charge of the Centre. His secretary ushered me into his office. I greeted the gregarious officer, "Good evening Sir."

"Yes, young man, why are you here? You are meant to be in your room and maintain the social distancing protocol."

"Sir, I'm here to lodge a formal complaint."

"What's the complaint about?"

"Sir, it's about an elderly woman who has been behaving funny since we got here."

"What's her problem?"

"I don't really know, but I suggest acute and chronic depression, Sir."

"Are you a doctor or a psychologist?"

"No Sir."

"Okay. We will handle it."

"Thank you Sir."

"You are welcome."

Within an hour, the officer and some of his aides came to attend to her.

The officer greeted her, "Madam, how are you doing?"

She kept quiet, but she was still looking into the sky.

"Madam, I'm greeting you."

"Don't greet me. You teamed up with my late husband to punish me and my daughter."

"Madam, are you okay?"

"I should ask you that question instead..."

"Madam you must maintain social distance here. Go to your room and rest. I learnt you have been here since morning."

"But you wicked people kept me in these chains and handcuffs. I don't have a room here. Free me, let me go home and rest. I can't rest in this prison."

The officer felt in his shirt pocket for a cigar and lighted it. He blew a plume of smoke. Being a smoker, his lips were dark like charcoal. He took a puff of his cigar.

"Can I have a stick of cigar too?" The woman asked.

"No, you need rest, not cigar."

"Who told you that? All my life, I have been smoking cigars."

"Okay then. I will give you a stick."

The officer handed her a stick of cigarette and lighted it for her. She was thankful.

"Madam, would you go to your room now?"

"Oh yes!"

She was ushered into her room.

In the middle of the night, the old woman started screaming and crying uncontrollably. Some of us got so bothered for her and I decided to lead a group of passengers to interface with the new officer who took over from the first officer who helped her earlier. The new one was not aware of her condition.

"This is an odd hour Sir..." I started, "... this woman's case is getting out of hand. We need a solution, Sir."

"May I appreciate all of you for showing concern. That's kind of you. Let's go and see her right away."

We followed him. On getting to the old woman's room, we saw that she had scattered her room beyond recognition. She was pacing back and forth. The officer tried to calm her but to no avail. I asked the officer, "Sir, don't you think this quarantine or imprisonment is hugely affecting her thinking which is causing her severe levels of depression?"

"I beg your pardon! This place is not a prison!"

"Sorry Sir. However, the psychological impact on each of us varies. Maybe the quarantine experience is a frightening and depressing one."

"Are you a psychologist?"

"No Sir."

 "Coming here terrified me," a fellow passenger said.

"But why? It's really not as scary as it seems or as people paint it."

About five of us stood there watching the woman performing her drama.

"Please, has this woman eaten dinner?" The officer asked me.

"Not really. Maybe, junk food. I saw her cracking biscuits in the evening."

"Madam, would you like to eat some food?

She responded, "It is time for breakfast... Please serve me cereal, tea and sandwiches."

"Okay, we will do that just in a few minutes. But I want you to sit down or lie down on your bed..."

"I like to watch TV," the old woman requested.

The officer turned the TV on for her.

"Madam, which channel do you prefer?"

"Comedy channel, let me laugh away the agony of this prison..."

The officer turned to me and asked, "Why do you people call the Centre a prison?"

"It's because of the restrictions or lack of freedom here," I responded

"And the fact that we are forced to be here... Prisoners are usually forced against their will," another passenger chipped in.

The officer asked for a volunteer that could stay with the woman having significant psychological difficulty. I volunteered. And I was left alone with her. But she turned inward and even became more or less paranoid. I tried to strike a conversation with her but my efforts ended in vain. I concluded that she was depressed, as such, she must be attended to by a professional psychologist. A Centre like this must have professional care-givers!

In the morning, the woman was given an exemption. The officer made contact with her relatives who promptly came to pick her up. But a mild drama ensued. The woman said she was not leaving the Centre until I was given exemption too. She insisted that I must be freed with her.

The officer explained to her, "Madam, your case is different, that's why we are giving you an exemption. This man will stay here for fourteen days."

"No! No! I will not go! Let me stay here and eat free food. Ghanaian government must feed me for free. The government is owing me money. My retirement benefits are still pending..."

The officer was confused, not knowing what to do. He phoned a superior officer for a consultation about the woman's case.

After his phone call, the officer turned to me and declared, "Young man, I'm pleased to inform you that your volunteering job has earned you exemption too. You may go home. But you must be self-isolated in your house for the remaining days. We will keep in touch with you daily to check on you. Congratulations and good luck..."

Thank you Sir. I'm so grateful. This is an unusual favour..."

"Go and thank the old woman who insisted that you must be released with her..."

"Yes, I will."

"One good turn deserves another! You volunteered to keep her company. Now it's your turn to reap your goodness..."

"That's a law of Karma for you. It pays to plant the good seed in life!" A colleague to the officer interjected.

CHAPTER

Seventeen

Without hesitation, I called my wife to break the good news of my exemption to her. She was evidently enthralled. I informed her of my intention to commence my journey back to Tamale without further delay. But she suggested, "My dearest, it will be gratifying to visit and spend the night with your friend, Moses. Tomorrow will be ideal for you to journey back to Tamale. How do you see that?"

"Oh yes, it's a delightful suggestion! I didn't even think of visiting my friend before coming over. Poor me, poor manners..."

"My dear, you are not poor. And you don't have poor manners!"

"I'm sorry. I understand..."

"Mind your words always... with words you attract things into your life."

"Oh yes! Spot-on, my dearest damsel. And how is our baby?"

"He is kicking fine. He is waiting for you, my EDD is this week or next."

"Wow! It will be a remarkable thing to watch you bring forth my baby."

"Can you stand the labour ward?"

"Yes, I can. You need my support... By God's grace, I should be hitting the road to Tamale tomorrow... Very early in the morning!"

"Okay. Till you come."

"I will call you later. Okay?"

"Okay. Stay safe dear. Bye..."

"Bye, my dearest damsel. I love you."

"I love you too."

A few minutes later, I called Moses that I was on my way to his place. He responded with delight and excitement: "Pumaya, what's happening? You are meant to be there for fourteen days..."

"My friend, watch out for an interesting story about my release..."

"Okay. I can't wait to see you. Are you taking Uber?"

"Yes. I'm inside one already."

"Okay, that's splendid. I'm indoors tidying up my apartment."

My friend and I had a wonderful reunion, even as I apprised him about all that transpired at the Quarantine Centre. He laughed out loud at the old woman's behaviour, and he wondered if she was actually ill or she was just pretending. I also briefed him about the high points of the training. No doubt, I was splendidly impacted, especially in the area of interpersonal relationships. Before the training, my social skill was abysmally low. But now, I could boast of having people skills and relating to people with minimal conflict. And my prayer and fasting life has improved appreciably. Moses was happy for me and I thanked him for his support and encouragement.

I told him about one of our instructors, Mr Adekinki who added so much value to us. I loved the man and his mannerisms. While lecturing, he used to touch his nose intermittently. He also used to pull his trousers as if the trousers were falling off his buttocks.

This lecturer came to class the first day of lectures and thundered, "Abraham armed his trained servants! Do you hear me? No training, no arming! So you are here to be trained in order to be armed. How many of you want to be armed? You need to be trained first! There is nothing that enhances or boosts victory and success in life like training!"

During a certain class, a student, Jerome Okplogidi raised his left hand to take permission. And the lecturer asked him, "Mr Man... Why didn't you raise your right hand?"

And his funny answer was, "Sorry Sir, my right hand is sick."

"How can your right hand be sick?" The lecturer asked.

"Sorry Sir, my right hand is paining me..."

"Better! You need to improve your English. Okay?"

"Okay Sir."

"You may go."

As he was going out of the class, the student farted. And the whole class shouted, "Bombshell! Bombshell! Bombshell!"

"Moses! My course mates are a bunch of funny folks. I will surely miss them..."

"Pumaya, I can see that you had an awesome time," Moses interjected.

"Yes, I did."

"What about other lecturers?"

"Ahh! That's a week-long storytelling session. If I start talking about Mr Jasper Okoko and his wife, and other side attractions, we will not sleep tonight... Moses, the truth is that the story of my adventure in Lagos will not end in one month or in a year. It's a life-long story..."

"I can imagine."

Early in the morning, the following day, Moses accompanied me to the park where I took a vehicle to Tamale. Coincidentally, I boarded the same vehicle that brought me to Accra on my way to Lagos, three months earlier. The driver recognized me and both of us exchanged pleasantries.

About twenty or so kilometres from Accra Motor Park, a passenger started shouting, "Driver stop! Park! Driver Park!..."

We were scared as we thought he was a robber. So all of us responded in unison, "Driver, don't stop. Driver, don't stop. Keep moving..."

The young man shouted the more, "Driver stop! Stop! I want to ease myself..."

"Control yourself, I can't stop here!" The driver responded angrily.

The young man kept screaming, "Please stop! Stop!"

"I can't stop! This place is dangerous. Let me move to a more secured place. Hold yourself."

"No! I can't hold myself. It is coming..."

"What is coming? Do you want to deliver a baby?" We all giggled.

Before the driver could reach a more secured place, the young man defecated. He soiled his trousers with foul-smelling faeces. It was a very humiliating moment for the young handsome man who was gloating or swaggering at the motor park. He stepped out of the van feeling so ashamed and embarrassed. A lady in our vehicle offered him a toilet paper and water to clean himself up. She also gave him perfume to deodorize his trousers. Throughout our journey to Tamale, the young man kept to himself. I felt sorry for him. I wanted to give him a pair of trousers, but the guy was huger and taller than me.

Without much hassles on the way, we arrived Tamale at 7 p.m. thereabout. My wife, mother and brothers were at the motor park awaiting my arrival. The moment they sighted me, they all jumped on me in heartfelt excitement. With tears dripping down from my eyes, I embraced my wife. She whispered to me, "My dear, welcome back. Your boy is coming..."

"Are you due?"

"Yes, I am. I'm in labour..."

"Let's rush to the hospital then..."

Pronto, I appealed to the driver who brought me from
Accra to assist us to the hospital. I told him that my wife
was in labour. He gladly obliged me. And we set out for
the hospital in a hurry. On arrival, my wife was wheeled
into the labour ward. My mother and brothers were not
allowed into the ward, but as her husband, I was allowed
to accompany her. The labour ward was a different
terrain or experience altogether. There were many
women crying and wailing profusely due to labour pain.

My wife's labour pain was acute, intense, harrowing and
unbearably excruciating. She was moaning and wailing
like other women at the stage of delivery. But steadily, I
kept pacifying her. The chief midwife of the Tamale
Government Hospital was pleasant and supportive as she
kept coming and going, checking up on my wife. She
even instructed a junior midwife to keep an eye on her.

Within an hour or so of labour, my wife delivered a baby
boy. The chief midwife who took the delivery instantly
placed our baby on my wife's chest, and said, "Madam!
... Congratulations! You made it."

She turned to me and said, "Mr Abdulai, well done and congratulations! You have a clone, a replica here..."

"Madam Midwife, thank you so much. I'm grateful. We are most grateful," I responded joyfully.

"Don't bother... We are simply doing our job."

Promptly, I dashed out from the labour ward to announce the good news of our baby's arrival to my mother and brothers. Together, we all started thanking God and jubilating.

9 789785 666892